CLAIMED

By

Em Brown

CLAIMED

CHAPTER ONE

BRIDGET

Present

"I'm not sure I'm ready to date," I say to Lashawna as we stand amid a pile of shoes that others had left on the floor of Nordstrom Rack.

My friend Lashawna hands me a pair of strappy four-inch heels.

I balk. "Won't these shoes send the wrong message?"

"Like what?" Lashawna asks, examining a pair of espadrilles for herself.

"That I'm willing to go to third base on the first date—which I'm not."

"Sure, they have a little come-and-get-me vibe, but that doesn't mean you're going to put out. This is the 21st century, Laney."

"Women still get judged as sluts if we try to look too sexy."

"By older generations, maybe. Since when were you so old-fashioned in your thinking?"

Since *not* being "old-fashioned" landed me in a relationship with a gangster.

But Lashawna, even though she's my first and closest friend in Denver, doesn't know my past. She doesn't even know my real name, Bridget Moore, or that my real hair color is light brown instead of black. With my hair dyed darker, I look more like my father, whom Grandma liked to say is even cuter than Michael B. Jordan. Otherwise, I'm a blend of both my parents. I have my mom's hazel eyes but not her blond hair, and I have my dad's smile. According to Grandma, who raised me, I have my dad's temperament, too.

"I'm a mom," I answer, picking up a more modest pair of shoes instead.

"So?" Lashawna challenged, taking the shoes from me and replacing them on the rack. "That doesn't mean you can't be sexy. You could totally be a MILF. Look at you. You just need a new wardrobe."

I glance down at my Vans, which are now officially gray instead of white, but I thought they were a good find at the local Goodwill since they were my size and already broken in. As a single mother trying to put herself through nursing school, I have zero extra cash for improving my wardrobe.

"Besides, you're only twenty-four," Lashawna continued. "Too young to be picking out granny shoes."

"I thought the shoes were nice," I mumble.

Lashawna had my age right, along with a few other details, like my son's real name. Evan Lowell was born at Denver Health a year and a half ago, seven months after I ran away from California to hide out in Colorado. Though it had been tough fitting everything I owned into two suitcases and leaving my education at UC Berkeley, I considered myself lucky that I had somewhere to go. I had Aunt Coretta. She's not actually related to me, but she feels like family since she was my grandmother's best friend and neighbor. I lived with Grandma, and Aunt Coretta had been a daily fixture in my life till she moved to Denver to look after her own grandbabies.

Lashawna grabs my hand. "Come on, let's find a dress to match those shoes."

Within minutes, she's found a black sheath misplaced behind a rack of coats. Lashawna goes to nursing school with me, but she has a sharp eye for fashion.

"This will look amazing on you," she says. "And it's not too slutty, so your mom sensibilities won't be offended."

I look over the sheath and have to agree. Taking it from her, I examine the size. Four. I used to be able to fit into that size without problem, but after I stopped breastfeeding Evan, I put on a few pounds.

"It's too small," I tell Lashawna. If we can't find a suitable outfit, that'll be my excuse for rescheduling the date.

Undaunted, Lashawna pushes me toward the dressing room. "Try it on. You never know."

Inside the dressing room, I take off my shorts and t-shirt. With a limited income while juggling school, raising Evan, and working as a cashier at Target, my wardrobe is about what's inexpensive and comfortable. After taking off the Vans, I slide into the heels and pull the sheath over my head.

Lashawna knocks on the dressing room door. "I wanna see."

"I'm going to bust a seam," I say as I open the door.

Lashawna beams. "Damn, you look good, girl. Just put some Spanx underneath and you're good to go."

"Spanx is out of my budget."

"We'll find something."

I shake my head. "You're so enthusiastic, you should be the one going on the date."

"Well, Josh *is* cute," she says of the guy who'd ended up sharing a table with me, Lashawna and our classmate Maria at our favorite coffee shop last week because the place was packed and we had a table of six to ourselves. "He kind of reminds me of Ryan Gosling. But no way am I spoiling your opportunity."

"Honestly, I wouldn't mind. I've had so much going on in my life, I haven't thought about men or dating in a long time."

She raises a brow. "Not thought about men? I've seen the way you look at Gerald in our microbio class."

"So he's good-looking." *And safely gay.* I add, "It doesn't mean I want to date him. Besides, Josh doesn't know I have Evan."

"So tell him."

"Maybe I should let him know *before* the date. That way, we don't waste each other's time if he's not interested in dating a single mom."

"First, show him what he'd be missing out on if he didn't date you. Besides, you've got to do this for yourself and take that first step at some point."

"I was thinking after graduating would be a better time to start dating. Evan's not even two."

"You're always going to have an excuse. And cute guys like Josh aren't necessarily going to rain down on us once we graduate."

"But I feel guilty going on a date when Coretta took Evan for the weekend so that I could *study* for our final exam."

"Like you need to study. You always ace the tests. Drinks don't have to take long. *Carpe diem.*"

I let out a shaky breath. She's right. Maybe I should just go and conquer my fear.

"What's the worst that can happen?" Lashawna asks. "You find out he's not interested in children. So that means he's not Mr. Right. Next."

I vaguely hear what Lashawna says because, in my mind, I'm answering her question. The worst that can happen is that I fall in love with a man who's part of an international triad, my roommate gets murdered, and I have to skip town in the middle of the night because I might be the next victim.

"Hey, you okay?"

I realize I'm staring at Lashawna without actually seeing her. "Sorry, just...my last relationship was a disaster, so that's why I'm not eager to get back in the ring."

"I hear you. I'm sorry if I've been pushy. You and Josh would make such a cute couple, but if you're not ready, you're not ready."

I feel bad about disappointing Lashawna. I don't know if she intended to use reverse psychology on me, but it's working. I don't want my past mistake ruining the rest of my life. And my mistake was hardly intentional. I didn't go looking to date a gangster.

"Let's do this," I declare.

Lashawna lights up. "Great! Now that we've got your outfit

picked out, we just need to do something about your hair."

I touch my curls. Like my clothes, my hairstyles are about what's easy and comfortable. My hair has grown long because I prefer to save the money and cut it myself, except I haven't had any time. I didn't fully appreciate all that Grandma went through raising me until I had Evan. Even though I had thought long and hard about an abortion—who was I to be having a child while starting a whole new life?—Aunt Coretta talked me out of it.

"You're cut from the same cloth as your grandma," Coretta had told me. "If she can do it, you can, too. And look how good you turned out."

I don't know that I made the right decision in having Evan, but ever since he was born, I can't imagine life without him. Unlike my mom, who left me with Grandma, then went off to Europe to date Greek men and sail on their yachts, I was going to be there for Evan in every way.

My mom dropped me off with my paternal grandmother when I was still a baby. My father had died in action just a few months before while serving in Afghanistan, and Grandma didn't dispute my parentage even though she knew very little about my mother. My mom had admitted I was the result of a one-night stand she had had when rebounding from a previous relationship.

A part of me wishes my father had been a part of my life. I remember coming home from elementary school sad one day because my class had painted mugs for Father's Day and the teacher had told me I didn't have to make one. Grandma told me that of course I should make one, and she placed my finished mug next to the photo of my father she kept on the living room table.

I often wonder if Evan will grow up feeling an emptiness where his dad should be. I dread the day he grows up and asks who his dad is, but I don't know that I'll ever tell my son.

CHAPTER TWO

DARREN

Present

She looks hot in that black dress and those high-heeled shoes.

Damn.

I don't remember her ever wearing shoes like that for me.

From my car parked across the street, I watch Bridget walk into the restaurant. It took me more than two years to track her down, and she's so close, I can hardly wait another second to confront her. To see the look on her face when she sees me. What will her reaction be? I don't delude myself into thinking she'll be happy to see me. She left me for a reason, and whatever that reason is, I doubt it's changed.

I'd be satisfied with mortification.

Because she knew better. I didn't give her permission to leave.

So now I'm taking her back.

Whether she likes it or not, she's mine.

CHAPTER THREE

BRIDGET

Present

"And this is Evan having watermelon for the first time," I say, showing a pic on my cellphone to Josh as we sit at the bar of the restaurant. "It's his favorite food now."

Josh smiles politely. I can't tell if he's repulsed or not to find out I have a kid.

"Can I get you a real drink?" he asks, nodding toward my club soda.

"I'm good," I reply. "Alcohol messes with my sleep, and I need a good night's rest whenever I can get it."

Josh hasn't asked about Evan's father. Maybe he doesn't want to get jealous. Or maybe he's not that interested in Evan.

He reaches for my glass and takes a sip. "How can you drink this stuff without alcohol?"

"I'm used to it. Sometimes I'll have it with grenadine."

"Like a Shirley Temple?"

"I know, it's a kid's drink. But for me, it beats waking up five, six times in the night."

"Then let's get you a Shirley Temple. At least it beats a plain old soda."

He waves at the bartender and orders the drink.

"I've got a few more pics of Evan on my phone," I venture. Actually, my phone is full of photos of Evan, but I don't plan on showing them all to Josh. I just want to see his response.

He flashes that gorgeous smile at me, the one that had us all swooning at the coffee shop. "Let's see 'em," he says.

Encouraged, I show him the photo of Evan snuggling with the neighbor's puppy, Evan covered in spaghetti, and Evan curled in Aunt Coretta's lap.

"Cute," Josh says.

But his statement rings a little hollow. I can't say for sure, but I'm not getting the same vibe that I did when I first met him. At the coffee shop, he was in full charm mode. Tonight, he just doesn't seem as interested.

We talk about the usual date topics: his line of work, my studying nursing, how long we've each lived in Denver, etc. But as I finish the Shirley Temple, I'm more and more convinced that I'm not Ms. Right for him, and he's not Mr. Right for me. I try not to think about how much I spent on the shoes and dress.

"Oh, man," Josh says after reading a text that just came into his cell. "My grandfather's in the hospital. I have to go. I am so sorry about this."

Somehow, I can't help but wonder if that's what the text really was about.

"Yeah, yeah, of course," I answer.

He stands up. "I owe you dinner. Maybe next Saturday."

"Don't even worry about it."

"I'll text you."

Sure, you will, I can't help but think. Oh well. At least I can tell Lashawna I tried. This way, I'll make it back in time to read Evan *Good Night, Moon* over FaceTime.

I check the time on my phone, a photo of Evan pointing up at a butterfly as my home screen. It's a recent photo. The older he gets, the more he looks like his father.

A shiver runs down my spine. I've gone days, even weeks without thinking of Darren. But for some reason, I've thought of him multiple times today and yesterday. Maybe going out on the date is what's stirring up old memories.

CHAPTER FOUR

BRIDGET

Past

"Please, please, please, please," begs Amy Liu, my junior-year roommate at Cal. We share a two-bedroom apartment just off campus with our friend Simone and a transfer student named Kat.

"What about Simone? She'd go with you in a heartbeat," I reply. I've made myself comfortable on my bed with my statistics textbook and don't feel like budging, especially to go all the way into the city.

"She's at a poetry reading."

"What about Kat?"

"She's rushing Delta Delta Gamma. Tonight's the weigh-in."

I roll my eyes. Rumor has it that Delta Delta Gamma has all the prospectives stand on a scale to be weighed. After that, they get a number written on their foreheads for the number of pounds they have to lose before they can be accepted.

"Please. You have no idea how hot this guy is," Amy continues about the guy she served at the fancy restaurant where she works. "He didn't leave his number, so showing up at this club is the only way I'll get to see him again."

I purse my lips. It's late. I need to finish a problem set for statistics. But I can't let Amy go stag at some club in the city.

I make one final attempt to stay. "But this guy knows you work at the Golden Garden."

"I told him I'd show up, and if I don't, he might think I'm not interested."

"You think he'd give up that easily?" I ask. It's hard for me to imagine because Amy is gorgeous. Like, movie-star-glamour beautiful. Her brows, always professionally done, have the perfect arch. She doesn't need to wear fake lashes to enhance her looks, but she does anyway. Her brand-name clothes show off her slender figure, and she has thick hair lightened with blond highlights.

"I'm sure he doesn't have a shortage of women after him. Please, Bridget. I'll help you with all your stats assignments."

I close my textbook. "Don't worry about it. I'll go with you."

With a squeal, Amy hugs me. "Thank you, thank you, thank you! I just need fifteen or twenty minutes to change."

"Change? You can't go as is?"

"This club could be swank. I don't want to be underdressed."

I look down at my baggy sweats. "Do I have to change?"

Her eyes widened. "Yes, please."

I don't exactly have clubbing clothes, but I find a pair of black jeans and a cold-shoulder blouse. However, they don't meet Amy's approval.

"I wish you could fit into one of my skirts," she says as she zips into skin-tight leather pants.

I'd have to be half my size to do that.

"But maybe you could wear my wraparound halter."

Her top is a little tight and short on me, exposing my midriff.

"Sexy," she pronounces. "Now what are you going to do for shoes?"

"My fake Uggs?"

She frowns. "You can't wear shoes like that to a club!"

"It's going to be freezing in the city at this time of night. And there's no way I can fit into any of your tiny shoes."

Amy sighs.

"All I have are my flip-flops," I say, pulling them from my closet. "There's a little bit of bling on them. It's that or my sneakers."

Amy releases another sigh. "I guess we'll have to go with the boots."

I grab a chunky button-up sweater to wear over the halter. I don't know how Amy plans to stay warm in her lacy camisole top and strappy gold sandals.

"Do you think these bangles are too much?" she asks, bracelets jangling as she holds up her arm. Her sapphire ring, an heirloom from her great-grandmother, which Amy never takes off for any reason except to get it cleaned, catches the light.

I don't own jewelry except for a few pairs of earrings, so I'm not the best judge, but I tell her honestly that she looks amazing.

"If I were gay, I would totally be hitting on you right now," I add.

As we walk down the stairs, we come across Keira and Jordan, seniors who live in the unit above us.

"Wow, Amy, you look fab," Kiera remarks. She turns to me, looks over my ensemble and smirks. Kiera's not a fan of me ever since I told her on move-in day that her cardboard boxes could go in the recycling bin instead of the trashcan.

"You must be going someplace special," Jordan says.

"The Lotus, a club in San Francisco."

Jordan's eyes widen. "No way."

"You've heard of it?"

Jordan tosses back her long golden curls. "Of course I have. I know all the exclusive places in the city."

I don't doubt her. She grew up in Pacific Heights, the daughter of some cosmetics tycoon. And as if she doesn't think she's hot stuff already, she's currently dating the football team's starting quarterback, who's expected be a first-round draft pick in the NFL. She's not a fan of me, either. I'd say it's probably because I once asked her to turn down her music while I was studying for a midterm, but I don't think she's a fan of anyone who doesn't hold the same social status as she does.

"Oh, so you've been there. What's it like?" Amy asks.

Jordan's face darkens. "There's no way you're getting into The Lotus."

"I got an invite from JD Lee."

"I don't even know who that is."

"So what's The Lotus like?" I inquire deliberately.

She tosses her hair again. "I have my favorite clubs already, so I've never felt the need to go to The Lotus."

Meaning you've never received an invitation. But I keep my mouth shut because Grandma raised me to be nicer than that.

Now I'm slightly more interested in checking out this club with Amy.

We take the BART train into San Francisco and get off at the Powell Street station. Although I'd prefer to hoof our way to the club to save on cab fare, I doubt Amy will want to walk seven blocks in her sandals. And as I predicted, the city is chilly. Even though Berkeley is only about ten miles across the bay, it's a different climate. Amy's bare arms would freeze off by the time we arrived at the club.

"I'll pay for the cab," Amy offers as she flags one down.

I decide to look up this club, The Lotus. Oddly, nothing comes up. No website, no Yelp reviews.

"You sure you got the name right?" I ask Amy as the cab drives in the direction of Chinatown.

"Trust me, I would not forget anything this guy says," Amy replies.

"Wow, you've got it bad for him. What's his name again?"

"Jin Dao Lee, but he goes by 'JD.'"

"Have you looked him up on the internet?" I ask, now dying of curiosity to see what this guy looks like.

"Of course. I mean, I tried, but he doesn't have a profile anywhere. I couldn't find him on Twitter or Facebook or the usual places. He might be on one of the Asian apps, though."

On the outskirts of Chinatown in what might be Nob Hill, the cab pulls up in front of a four-storied building that looks like it's made entirely of black glass. There's no sign outside bearing the name of the club.

"Are you sure this is it?" I ask, surprised that a club would be located on such a quiet street.

"This is the address you gave me," said the driver, pointing to his GPS screen.

Amy and I get out and walk through glass double doors into a dark lobby with what looks like an expensive rug covering gleaming marble floors. Behind two large bouncers are another set of doors, through which I can hear music thudding.

"Cellphones, keys, and electronics," says a security guard standing beside the metal detector.

I haven't been to that many clubs, but I don't remember ever seeing a metal detector at one before. After placing my cell in a basket and passing through, I reach for my cell but get handed a number instead.

"We keep everything until you leave," he explains.

"Seriously?"

"No photos allowed."

I suppose a place like this is unlikely to try to steal our phones from us. Amy and I pocket our numbers and walk up to the bouncers.

"Name and ID," says the one with the shaved head.

Amy pulls out her driver's license. "Amy Liu."

He eyes me with skepticism. "Who's your friend?"

"Bridget Moore."

The guy looks over my ID and checks a handheld digital device. "Your name's not on the list."

"I told JD I'd probably bring a friend," Amy explains.

He talks into his headset and looks up to a security camera pointed at us. "Got a Bridget Moore with Amy Liu."

After a very long pause, I begin to think that Jordan's right about the exclusivity of this place. Finally, a response comes through on the other end of his headset, and the bouncer waves us through.

Amy grabs my hand as we walk past the two bouncers. I can tell she's trying to hold in her excitement. Two doormen open the doors for us and we step into a cavernous room with lighting that slowly fades into different shades of blue. Based on the size of the building I saw when we were outside, there's more to the place than what I currently see. I figure the other part of the building is just office space.

A winding staircase to our right leads to balconies on the second and third floors. The balconies are tucked into shadows and don't have any lighting except for what appear to be votive candles. Nearly as high as the second balcony are some dance platforms. A woman wearing a lace-up corset and skin-tight leather shorts dances provocatively on one platform, and on another, a man and woman with equally scant clothing grind hips together.

"May I take your sweater?" asks a woman in a knockout red dress. She has on a little hat that reminds me of one worn by a flight attendant on an Asian airline brochure that Amy once had.

"I'm good," I reply.

Amy tells her we're looking for JD Lee.

"He's not here yet," the attendant says.

Seeing a bar just off the dance floor, Amy says to me, "Let's grab a drink."

I don't turn twenty-one for another two months, but even if I were old enough to drink, I'd probably just ask for a lemonade.

We walk past tables toward the bar. Seeing how dressed up everyone is, I begin to rethink my attire choice. Oh well. Nothing I can do about it now.

"Should I order a sex-on-the-beach or is that too much of a college drink?" Amy whispers to me as we climb onto the barstools.

I shrug my shoulders.

"I'll have a mojito with extra mint," Amy tells the bartender.

"Coke," I answer when he turns to me.

"With rum, vodka, Jack?" he asks.

"Straight Coke."

"You could've ordered a real drink," Amy says. "He didn't ask for ID."

"I like Coke."

I hope this JD Lee shows up soon as I consider how late it'll be when I make it back home.

Amy presses a finger to her eyelid. "I think one of my lashes is coming off. I'm going to find the restroom. Be back in a minute."

I watch her hop off the stool as the bartender sets our drinks down.

"Straight Coke," he says with a smile. He seems like a nice guy and the only one in the place who hasn't given me a skeptical look.

"Thanks."

A glass of soda at a place like this probably costs ten times what I'd pay from a vending machine. I sip the Coke slowly to make it last longer. Besides, I need the drink to distract me from the looks I'm getting.

CHAPTER FIVE

DARREN

Past

"What the hell is that thing?" asks Kimberly Park, an ex-lover of mine who's now dating my cousin's friend.

Olga, a Russian blond bombshell, joins her at the balcony railing. "That is the ugliest sweater I have ever seen."

"So gross," Kimberly concurs before turning to where I'm sitting on a chaise lounge. "You should have your manager take care of this. You don't want people thinking the club's rep is going downhill. Don't you have important company coming tonight?"

I rub my temple, unsure I'm up for a night of Kimberly's nitpicking. It's been a rough day with a close friend of mine getting arrested this morning on racketeering charges, and Lee Hao Young, an Operations Officer—also known as a Vanguard, and ranked just below the Dragon Master of the *Jing San* Triad—is in town from China and coming to The Lotus.

Plus, it's hard for me to imagine how Kimberly and Olga could get so worked up. Anyone lucky enough to be allowed into my club dresses to impress. And while not everyone can look as hot as Kimberly and Olga, both lingerie models, no one can look *that* bad.

But I stand corrected.

After joining the women at the railing, I see in an instant what they're talking about. The taupe-colored sweater the woman at the bar is wearing *is* the ugliest sweater. I look around for Cheryl, my manager, but don't find her.

"And what's with the snow boots?" Kimberly shivers in disgust. "How did she get past your bouncers? Is this a joke? Where's Cheryl? Isn't your important company going to be here soon?"

"I'll take care of it," I tell her, "though it's not like you're going to go blind from looking at someone who's only half as hot as you."

"A *half?*"

"He means a tenth," Olga supplies.

"What she said," I say as I head down the stairs.

Kimberly might be right about this patron being a joke of some kind. I'd put my money on Ronald Ho. Like me, Ronald is twenty-eight years old, but he stopped maturing emotionally at thirteen. He said he was going to get me good after I neglected to get him tickets for the playoffs at Levi's Stadium. Except pulling a joke on a night when Lee Hao Young is going to be here is taking things too far.

On the ground floor, I'm stopped by patrons who want to talk to me: Jack Chiu, a lieutenant and one of our fixers in the SFPD; Marsha Holmes, a woman who handles my overseas accounts; and Adam Feinstein, a criminal lawyer whom many of my relatives keep on retainer. After telling each of them to schedule something with my manager/personal assistant, I check the time on my Audemars Piguet. Lee Hao Young could be here any minute.

"Hi," I say to the ugly-sweater woman.

"Hi," she responds, her eyes brightening for a second before giving me a wary look as if I might be some predator.

She can't possibly think I'm trying to pick up on her? I stand next to her at the bar and nod at Felipe, the bartender.

"What's the game?" I ask, noticing there's a second drink near her. Mojito with extra mint. Ronald's favorite.

She gives me a strange look "Excuse me?"

"Does Ron have a photographer planted in here?"

She frowns. "I'm sorry, you have me mixed up with someone else."

She's good. Much better than the actor Ronald hired to pretend to be an ex-lover of JD's to scare the shit out of the woman JD managed to steal away from Ronald at a party last year.

"You can give it up," I tell her. "Ron knows I don't allow any photos to be taken at The Lotus, so you can just pack it up and call it a night."

She looks at me like I've got a screw loose and glances around the club, probably looking for Ronald.

I lean in toward her. "Look, I admit it's funny. Kind of. The outfit's a real winner. I couldn't have picked out better. Kimberly's worried she's going blind just looking at the sweater."

The young woman's eyes widen. She glances over at Felipe as

if seeking help, but he goes back to wiping the counter.

"Did you come over here just to insult me?" she asks. Even in the dark, I can see her cheeks turning color. She's actually much better looking up close. It's the frumpy clothes that make her look less than impressive. "What kind of an asshole are you?"

Now I'm starting to get a little impatient. "The kind of asshole who doesn't put up with shit like this. I've got important company coming tonight."

For a second, I almost believe her mortification is real.

I lower my tone. "You can drop the act and go put on some real clothes now. Try your stunt some other night."

The next thing I know, I have Coke dripping down my face and onto my silk Versace button-up shirt.

Felipe is near me in an instant with a clean towel. I wipe my face and see the sweater woman has walked away. I'm about to storm after her with the intention of tossing her out myself when I find a petite young woman standing at my elbow.

"What did you say to my friend?" she exclaims.

I wipe my face. "Who are you?"

"Amy—oh."

Her pupils dilate after I drop the towel. I know that look. It's the kind of look I'm used to getting from women. The kind of look I *didn't* get from the ugly-sweater woman. Surprisingly.

"Amy Oh?" I echo.

"Amy Liu. I was invited here by JD."

I raise a brow. "JD Lee."

"Yeah, you know him?"

"I do."

I think through ugly-sweater woman's reactions to everything I had said. Maybe they were real after all. I look over Amy from head to toe. She's cute, petite and young enough to look like jailbait. Exactly the kind JD goes after.

"You know Ronald Wong?" I ask her.

She shakes her head. I believe her.

"Who's your friend?" I ask.

"Bridget Moore."

Now, I know JD wouldn't have invited ugly-sweater lady.

As if reading my mind, Amy adds, "I asked her to come with me since I've never been here before."

Behind the bar, Felipe is trying to hide his grin. I throw my towel at him.

"Whatever they want is on the house," I tell him.

My residence is on the fourth floor of the building. There, I rinse the soda out of my hair, run fresh hair gel through it, wash my face and put on a new shirt. I decide to wear a vest and jacket for Lee Hao Young. Having lived only in the US, I sometimes forget that those from the mainland tend toward formal.

"OMG, we saw what happened!" Kimberly says when I return to the second-floor balcony. "You should have had Marshall with you!"

"I don't need a bodyguard for everything I do," I remind her as I sit down.

Cheryl comes up to me and hands me a glass of bourbon. "I heard what happened. I shouldn't have allowed the woman in. I'll have her thrown out once we locate her."

"I saw her go into the restroom," Olga said. "I can see that ugly sweater a mile away."

"No, she stays," I say. "She's with JD. Sort of."

Kimberly's eyes pop out. "What?!"

"Don't look at her if she bothers you so much."

"I won't. I can only take so much ugly in one night."

I almost protested that sweater woman wasn't actually ugly. Her eyes were bright and attractive. Her lips fairly full. With a little makeup and a better hairstyle, she could be on the upper end of the beauty scale.

I down the bourbon, unsure why I'm thinking about how this Bridget Moore looks.

"Your guest, Amy Liu, is here," I tell my cousin when he arrives with Eric Drumm, Kimberly's boyfriend. "Where's Hao Young? I thought he was coming with you?"

"We wrapped up business at dinner, and he wanted to call it a night. He went back to his hotel," JD replies as he tosses the spikey bangs that are always falling into his eyes.

I glance over at Eric and Kimberly, lip-locked by the railing. I'm not a huge fan of Eric, the son of a billionaire real estate developer who's currently governor of Florida and running for president, because he seems far too eager to ingratiate himself with members of the triad but plays it off like he's doing us a favor by blessing us with his company. Kimberly knows I only tolerate him because JD might want to go into a business venture with him, and I suspect my lack of enthusiasm for the guy is one of the reasons she's decided to date him.

"So where's Amy?" JD asks as he accepts a beer from one of the servers.

"You sure she's not jailbait?" I ask as Olga curls up next to me and plays with one of the buttons on my vest.

"Not likely. She says she's a junior at Cal."

"She brought a friend."

"Yeah, sorry about that. I told Cheryl it was okay."

"She's down at the bar."

"Mind if I invite her up here?"

"Go ahead."

Olga starts kissing my neck. We've had sex twice before, and I stop at three. After that, you risk moving into the gray zone before relationship territory. Kimberly looks over and frowns. She and Olga pretend to be friends, but there's not much love lost between them. I don't try to understand women's relationships with each other.

I consider spending the night with Olga, but I could also find a partner at the other part of the club.

For some reason, Sweater Woman comes to mind.

"I'll go down with you," I say to JD. "I owe the friend an apology."

Kimberly disengages from Eric's mouth. "You're not serious? The woman threw a drink in your face."

"I've had worse thrown at me."

"And since when do you apologize? Are you sure you even know how?"

The fact that she's Eric's girlfriend won't stop me from tying her down to the A-frame and spanking her till her ass is purple. But that might be exactly what she's after.

"I need the practice then," I say. My cell rings.

"I'll bring Amy and her friend up," JD tells me as I take the call.

It's Mitchell Lindsay, a state senator who wants to bring his mistress to the club tonight. He's received over $25,000 for securing government building contracts for various members of the *Jing San* and hopes to find additional ways to fund his bid for Secretary of State in two years.

"I'm sorry, Senator," I tell Lindsay, "I can only take so many newcomers at a time."

The FBI recently busted a state legislator up in Washington for racketeering, and I'm not entirely sure they don't have their eye on Lindsay. And since a lot of business gets conducted at The Lotus, the fewer outsiders, the better.

"You're going to let JD bring that ugly thing up here?" Kimberly asks when I'm done with the call.

I lean back and put my arm around Olga. "Get over yourself, Kim."

She scowls at me before turning to Eric. "Come on, the view's better on the third floor."

I watch her skinny ass sway as she stalks by.

"Let's talk later," Eric mouths to me.

I don't respond, though part of me thinks it would be amusing to wish him luck where Kimberly is concerned. My mother, who currently lives in Singapore, met Kimberly once and didn't like her, even though Kimberly was on her best behavior at the time.

"You can pick them better than that," my mother had scolded me. "Plenty of women out there with substance to go along with their putang."

I smile at how my mother suddenly talks urban when she really wants to make a point with me.

Olga reaches for my crotch again.

"Not now, babe," I say.

If I greet Miss Bridget Moore with a hard-on, I wouldn't be surprised to find myself covered in Coke again.

CHAPTER SIX

BRIDGET

Present

It feels cold, even though a heat wave is sweeping through Denver. But am I even in Denver still? I'm not sure how long I blacked out for.

Something like a black pillowcase wraps my head, so I can't see anything. I can't tell if it's light or dark. Based on the quiet around me, I'm guessing I'm indoors. But where, I have no idea. Thick tape covers my mouth, but even if I could scream, I'm not sure if it's a good idea to call attention to myself. My wrists are tied together and pulled overhead. I'm standing in my four-inch heels, shoes I knew I was going to be uncomfortable in, shoes that I splurged on for a date that went bust. And if I had never gone on that date, I wouldn't find myself in this situation.

The last thing I remember is being at the bar, my date apologizing that he had to go because he had just received a text that his grandfather was being taken to the hospital, me feeling both disappointed and relieved that the date had ended abruptly, the scent of incense as I climbed into the taxi, and…that's it.

I tug and twist my wrists about the ropes, but they hold tight.

Panicking won't help, but I'm scared to death. I try not to think about the worst that could happen and curse myself for watching one too many *Law and Order* episodes. Part of me wants to cry just imagining that I might never get to see Evan again. For Evan, I've got to figure a way out of this.

I pull again at the bonds until I get rope burn.

A door opens, and I freeze. Since I can't see anything, I have to rely on my sense of hearing. It sounds like a single set of footsteps walking toward me. My entire body tenses.

A hand cups my butt, and I try not to sob.

The hand moves lower, beneath my dress…between my thighs.

Okay, I can survive rape. Just don't kill me. Let me live so I can be there for Evan. Please.

I can't stop myself from whimpering. I start to hyperventilate when the door opens again. The hand between my legs is quickly gone.

"Did you just touch her?" a voice demands.

It sounds vaguely familiar, but I'm breathing too hard to hear properly.

"No! I was—"

I hear footsteps stomping toward me, a man grunting, brief scuffling, what sounds like a man being dragged along the floor, and then the door slamming shut.

I hear muffled voices—and then what sounds like a gun going off.

Shit! Shit, shit, shit, shit.

My body quakes from head to toe. I start yanking at the bonds. My desperation to be free is what keeps me from pissing myself.

This is bad. Very, very bad.

CHAPTER SEVEN

DARREN

Present

I stare at the asswipe lying on the floor clutching his leg where the bullet went in, blood seeping past his fingers. Grabbing his shirt, I pull him up enough so that he can look me in the eyes.

"Did I say you could touch her?" I demand.

"No, sir, no you didn't," he answers through clenched teeth.

I release his shirt. I don't want his blood getting on my Ferragamos or my dark-wash Stefano Ricci jeans. For a second, I contemplate shooting him in the balls. No one touches Bridge except me. Instead, I hand the gun back to Marshall.

"Get the son of a bitch out of here," I instruct.

Other members of my family would have killed for less, which makes me briefly question my fortitude, but I have more pressing things to consider. Squaring my shoulders, I go back inside the room where Bridge is tied to a thick reinforced pipe overhead. The roofie Josh slipped into her drink had worked well, knocking her out for the entire flight between Denver and California.

She senses my presence. I can see the tension in her body. My body, too, reacts. More than two years and I'm not any less immune to her.

Fuck.

I rake my gaze over her body. She looks as good as the last time I saw her, though I like her natural hair color better. I remember every curve, every inch. I know exactly how her skin will feel when I caress it. I know the sound she'll make when I fondle her clit. I know how hot her pussy will get when I sink my cock into her.

When I close my eyes, I can see the last time we played. It was at The Lotus. I had her tied in face-up horizontal suspension, her body mine to use as I pounded away into her cunt. In a short amount of time, she had developed a relatively high pain tolerance for rough fucking.

With her ankles and wrists shackled, spread-eagled, to either ends of a wooden beam hung from the ceiling, her most private parts were exposed and at my mercy. I'd paused to play with her clit, which I had pumped earlier till it swelled red and plump. Her head fell back, and she trembled.

"Look at me," I commanded.

Her gaze met mine, and I could see in her eyes the conflict between desire and fear of overwhelm. I fondled her clit a little harder while I sank my cock deeper. She started to writhe.

"Stay still," I ordered, pulling and pinching a nipple when she still squirmed.

Through her ball gag, she mumbled what sounded like, "I'm trying to."

For several minutes, I worked her clit and thrust into her wet heat while she tried to contain her trembling and straining as well as her growing need to come. She pleaded with her eyes for permission, then whimpered when I stopped caressing her clit to grab her thighs with both hands. I shoved myself into her, slowly so her body had time to swing back toward me. When my own needs became too hard to resist, I quickened my pace. Perspiration fell onto her mound. She didn't take her gaze off me, and looking into the brightness of her eyes is what sent me over the edge.

After the peak of my ecstasy had passed, I agitated her clit while my cock still throbbed hard inside of her.

"Please, may I come?" she asked.

I had heard her ask enough times to know that's what she said, even with the ball gag stuffed between her lips.

"Come," I answered.

She spasmed on my fading erection, shaking and bucking in the air. She cried against the gag, her lips parted wide, her brow intensely furrowed. I loved watching, hearing and feeling her come. In that moment, it was all I ever wanted in life: to give her pleasure. I wanted to give her anything and everything she wanted. I wanted to give her the world.

But that was then.

It's different now.

CHAPTER EIGHT

BRIDGET

Past

"OMG, did you see how *hot* that guy was?!" Amy squeals when I return to the bar after calming my nerves in the restroom. "He totally reminds me of Godfrey Gao. A clean shaven Godfrey, though Godfrey's stubble is totally sexy, too."

"You're talking about the guy who insulted me?" I ask, wanting to go home. That statistics problem set is what looks sexy to me right now.

"What did he say?"

"That I was ugly."

Amy's brows shoot up with amazement that someone would be that mean to a stranger.

The bartender sets a glass of Coke in front of me. "Everything's on the house tonight for you, ladies."

"Thanks," I say. "That's really kind of you."

"Boss' orders," he says.

"Oh, can I get another mojito then?" Amy asks. She hops onto the stool next to me.

I'm surprised security hasn't already come for me, but maybe the bouncers are busy and it's just a matter of time.

"Maybe you could apologize to the hottie."

I want to do what I can to help Amy out, but I balk at that. "I don't know. He was pretty damn rude. But if I get thrown out, I'll just wait for you outside."

"You want something else to go with your Coke?" the bartender asks after setting down the mojito for Amy.

"Maybe later," I reply, appreciating the bartender's act of courtesy, even if it's because he feels bad for me.

"You should get one of these," Amy says as she takes a long sip through the stirring straw. "They're so good."

"I don't think alcohol is going to help me figure out my calc problem set."

"Live it up a little, Bridget. We're in a super-exclusive club, everyone looks stunning—"

"Everyone except me."

Amy bites her bottom lip, then takes another sip of mojito.

"I know," I acknowledge. "You told me to wear something nice."

"Maybe if you took off that sweater…"

"Amy!" a man calls out.

A guy in his mid or late twenties walks up to us. This has to be JD. His jaw is less square but he has the same eyes as the guy who insulted me. I can see why Amy is swooning so badly. He has a boyish smile, his bangs hang long over his eyes—he keeps sweeping them back like some teenage heartthrob—and he's dressed immaculately. I don't know much about fashion, but I'm willing to bet his clothes and that gold bracelet around his wrist are expensive.

"So glad you came," he greets Amy.

Her eyes light up like diamonds at seeing him. "Me, too. This place is amazing," she gushes. "I brought a friend, Bridget. Hope you don't mind."

"'Course not. Hey, why don't we go up to the balcony. It's easier to talk there."

Amy eagerly hops off the barstool.

"I'll finish my Coke here, then join you guys," I say.

I watch as JD puts a hand on Amy's lower back and guides her to the winding staircase. The bartender comes over and takes Amy's glass.

"My sweater really that ugly?" I ask him.

He only smiles in return. I take off the sweater.

"That is better," he says in a tone so encouraging, I can't be upset at him for anything.

"The top actually belongs to my friend," I say. "I don't think I own anything swank enough for this place. Still, it was really rude of that guy to come up to me and say what he did."

"I heard. The boss thought it was Ronald pulling a prank."

I blink several times. "The boss?"

"Darren Lee. The club owner."

"I threw Coke at the club owner?" I ask.

The bartender smiles. "You sure did."

"He's not by chance related to JD Lee, is he?"

"They're cousins."

I drop my forehead to the bar. I can't believe this. My first time throwing a drink in someone's face and it turns out to be JD's cousin *and* the owner of the club? I'm getting thrown out for sure once the bouncers are done with whatever they're doing.

I thump my forehead against the top of the bar a few times. Maybe I've fallen asleep working on statistics and this is just a bad dream. I remain with my forehead pressed against the cool, smooth surface and release a breath.

"How does the bar look from there?"

I bolt upright because it's not the bartender speaking.

It's *him*.

Damn. He is super-hot. Which I had actually noticed the first time, but that all went away when he'd started talking. Even though part of me still feels like he deserved a Coke in the face, I start to apologize, only the words aren't coming out. Something about the way he's looking at me has me frozen.

"It...looks...fine," I answer. God, could I sound any stupider?

He looks amazing in his vest and jacket, like some haute couture model. It's obvious his fashion sense is superior to mine, but that still doesn't give him the right to be mean.

"I'm sorry I threw my drink in your face," I finally manage.

He doesn't respond right away and narrows his eyes. "Not really."

"What?"

"You're not really sorry."

In disbelief, I suck in my breath. "I'm not sorry?"

"Not really."

This guy was too much. "First you tell me I look bad, and now you're calling me a liar?"

"I didn't call you a liar. I just don't think your apology is all that sincere."

"You should appreciate that I said anything at all!" I blurt. My hand tightens around my glass of soda.

"So you admit you're not really sorry."

My jaw drops, but then I straighten. "Yeah. And even if I was really sorry, I'm not now!"

A vague grin seems to tug at the corner of his mouth. "Saying something untrue. Isn't that the definition of lying?"

I'm tempted to throw my second glass of Coke at him, but his hand grips my wrist before I can do anything. How the hell did he move so fast? And why is every nerve in my body on edge? For a moment, I can't do anything except fix on how firmly his hand holds mine down.

Slowly, he takes the Coke away with his other hand.

"I don't feel like changing again," he says, and several seconds pass before he releases me.

I don't know if it's anger or something else that has me frozen and unable to pick up the pieces of thought that his touch sent scattering. Part of me wants to walk straight out of the club, but I'm riveted to my spot by his stare. I have to look away if

I'm to have a chance at coherent thinking.

"You're only sorry because you found out I own the place and that I'm JD's cousin," he explains.

I bristle because he's right. If it weren't for Amy, I wouldn't have apologized. Not wanting to acknowledge his statement, however, I return, "Is this the sort of happy customer service you dole out here every night?"

"I don't get doused with Coke from my patrons every night."

"That only happened because you said what you did to me."

"I made a mistake. I'm sorry."

We stare at each for a beat.

"Not really," I reply.

He raises his dark brows.

"You're not really sorry," I parrot back.

His gaze hardens. Maybe he's the kind who can dish it but can't take it.

"I gave you drinks on the house, didn't I?"

I had forgotten that bit. Maybe we should call a truce. I don't want to be tempted to throw another Coke at him.

"Thank you," I say. "That was nice of you."

His expression softens and he slides my soda over to me. "You can have your drink back."

"I won't throw Coke at you again. I mean, you deserved it that first time. Even if you thought I was someone else, why would you say such mean things? Didn't your mom teach you any manners?"

He glances over at the bartender, who looks stunned and worried. I get the feeling no one talks to Mr. Haute Couture the way I just did. I regret letting my mouth run and decide to sip the Coke so I don't say anything else.

"And your mom taught you it's okay to throw drinks in people's faces?" Darren asks.

I take a long sip of my Coke, finishing the drink. "Touché."

"You can have something fancier than soda."

I think for a minute and turn to the bartender. "Can you do a Shirley Temple?"

"Dirty?" asks the bartender.

"Hunh?"

"With vodka."

"No, just a plain Shirley Temple."

"You got it. Boss?"

Mr. Haute Couture shakes his head. "You can have anything at the bar and you want a kids' drink?"

"I've got stats to get back to," I answer. "As you can see from how I'm dressed, and which you so kindly pointed out earlier, I'm not really here for clubbing. I'm here for my friend, Amy."

"You go to Cal with Amy?"

"Yeah, we're both juniors."

"Go Bears."

"Did you go to Cal?"

"I'm a Bruin."

"Oh. Amy calls it the University of Caucasians Lost Among Asians."

"Cute."

"Not really. I shouldn't have said that. It perpetuates the model minority myth. What did you study at LA?"

"Business Economics."

"Did you go on to business school?"

"No. The best education is provided by the real world."

Despite his pretty clothes, he definitely has an edge about him that suggests he might have taken a few courses from the school of hard knocks.

He's looking up at the third balcony. Following his gaze, I vaguely make out a woman with a dynamite figure. Behind her stands a man nuzzling her neck. I can't tell for sure, but it looks like she's staring at me.

Turning back to Darren, I ask, "How did you end up owning a club?"

"Wasn't comfortable at the other clubs. I wanted something that felt more like home."

"Have you always been in the club business?"

"No."

"Did you do something else before The Lotus?"

"I was in the family business."

"What was that?"

"Various things."

"Like what?"

"This an interrogation?"

I guess I *am* asking a lot of questions, but I didn't know what else to do since it seems like he isn't in a hurry to leave. I'm surprised he isn't.

"You can tell me about JD instead," I offer cheerfully. Maybe I can dig up something helpful for Amy.

"He's my cousin."

"I knew that already."

"What do you want to know then?"

I think for a moment. "What does he do?"

"He's in business."

"What kind of business?"

"The family business."

I sigh. This guy does not like to answer questions.

"Which is what?" I press.

"Import-export."

"What does he import or export?"

His face darkens for a second. "Mostly goods from China. What are you studying at Cal?"

I can't tell if he's trying to be polite in asking about me or because he doesn't want to talk about JD anymore.

I'm about to answer when I notice his jaw tightens. At first I'm confused because I can't see how I could have upset him, but then I see the woman from the third-floor balcony take the barstool next to him. Up close, she's even more gorgeous than Amy. Her hair is stylishly done, her brows perfectly manicured, her lips plump and red, her legs long and lean. The only knock against her is that she's a little on the skinny side, but otherwise she looks like she belongs on a fashion runway.

"What are you doing here, Kim?" Darren asks her. He doesn't seem all that pleased to see her.

"Thought I'd slum it, like you," she answers, flashing the whitest teeth I've ever seen.

I wonder what she means by slumming it.

She leans across Darren toward me. "Hi, I'm Kimberly."

"Bridget," I respond.

"Bridget. How cute. I didn't know people still named their kids that. Where's that sweater you were wearing?"

Before I can figure out what this woman's deal is, Darren is pulling me off my barstool. "Come on."

"Where are we going?" I inquire.

"The dance floor," he replies.

His hand is firmly at my back, pressing me forward, and I try not to let my brain fall to pieces again.

CHAPTER NINE

DARREN

Past

"Why are we going to the dance floor?" Bridget asks me as I guide her away from the bar.

Because if I let you hang around Kimberly much longer, she'll end up with Shirley Temple dripping down her face. Although part of me would find that amusing, I don't want to deal with Kimberly's reaction if that were to happen.

Instead, I reply, "To dance."

"I didn't say I wanted to dance."

Doesn't matter. In my world, what I say, goes. We're on the dance floor, and I pull her to me. "You have something better to do here?"

"Yeah, my Shirley Temple."

I stare down at her. Hundreds of women would die to be in her shoes right now, and she wants her fucking kids' drink? What's wrong with this woman?

I slide my hand up her back, between her shoulder blades. A small gasp escapes her lips. Now that's more of a reaction I expect.

She blinks several times. I don't think she knows what to say. She feels stiff and awkward in my arms, but she smells good. Not perfumed good. Just a hint of coconut soap or lotion.

Noticing that her arms hang at her sides, I ask, "You've danced before, haven't you?"

She gives me a look of disapproval, one that I'm fast becoming familiar with. "Of course I have."

With my arm about her waist, I yank her to me till there's barely an inch between us. Her arms fly immediately to mine, making sure our bodies don't touch further.

"The question I have is *why* are we dancing?" she asks.

I stare at her again. A few minutes beneath the paddle will stop all these questions. "You'd rather get to know my ex-girlfriend?" I retort.

She looks over at the bar, where Kimberly is frowning at us.

"I see. I'm your getaway car."

My brows lift. She clearly doesn't understand that I've done her a favor.

"I can handle Kimberly," I say. "I was trying to save you from getting chewed up and spit out by her. She can be nasty."

"Oh. Guess that's nice of you then."

That's a better response.

"Do you usually date women who are nasty?"

Suddenly, I'm picturing her cuffed to my St. Andrew's cross. Naked. Gasping as my flogger whips across her body.

"I'm not judging," she adds. "It's just a question, out of curiosity."

I turn it back on her. "You interested in the type of women I date?"

She studies me. "You can tell a lot about a guy by the women he dates."

"Can you?"

"Yeah." She furrows her brow. "Except there are some assholes who don't deserve the women in their lives. And the nice guys who must be masochistic because their girlfriends are total bitches." She studies me again. "So, if you like nasty women, either you're nasty yourself, or you're the masochistic nice guy."

Masochistic? Not really. Sadistic? Yes.

"Somehow, I don't think you're the latter," she determines.

"You say that just because I thought your sweater was ugly?"

She stares into my eyes, and for a moment, I think she sees everything about me. Every desire. Every secret. Every darkness.

She should be scared, but instead she seems…curious.

"Hey, don't see you on the dance floor often," a voice cuts in.

It's JD, and he has Amy with him. The young woman laughs and leans against him. Obviously drunk. She might have only had two drinks or so, but she's petite, so it probably doesn't take much alcohol to get her wasted.

"She get anything to eat?" I ask JD.

"Do the mint leaves in a mojito count?" JD responds.

Bridget looks at her friend with concern but says nothing. Within minutes, Amy and JD aren't so much dancing as they're making out, until Amy stumbles and backs JD into another couple.

"Maybe we should get something to eat," Bridget suggests.

"Yes, we should," I agree.

The four of us head upstairs to the balcony after Bridget grabs her drink and sweater from the bar. Kimberly is no longer there. I saw her on the ground floor talking to Harry Chen, a fashion designer and distant relative of mine.

A spread of lobster dumplings, abalone-topped shumai, oxtail xiao long bao with Sevruga caviar, and fresh mango and lychee await us.

"OMG," Amy gushes over the food.

Bridget's eyes also widen. JD opens a bottle of Moutai and sets down four glasses as I take a seat on my preferred chaise, where I can see everything below.

"Is that alcohol?" Bridget asks of the Moutai.

"Yeah, it's *baijiu*," JD answers.

"Thanks but I'll pass."

"You ever try *baijiu* before?"

"No, but I'm not twenty-one yet."

He stops pouring to look at her. "You're not serious?"

"Well, I turn twenty-one in two months."

"No, I mean you're not serious that you don't drink because you're not twenty-one yet?"

"Pretty much."

JD looks at me, stunned. He turns back to Bridget. "You're

55

joking."

"I've never seen her drink," Amy chimes in. "Even at frat parties."

"Who doesn't drink just 'cause they're not twenty-one yet?"

I sit back, mildly amused by JD's shock. I'm curious as to her answer.

"Are you like super religious or something? Like a Mormon?" JD asks.

"No. Just law-abiding," she answers.

"You're shittin' me. You know that most of the world's drinking age is like eighteen?"

"But it's twenty-one here."

"We're not going to card you."

"My grandma never had any about the house, and I just never developed an interest."

JD looks over at Amy, who shrugs. He hands her a glass. "Well, this is good stuff. We got to break you in. You're missing out."

"She should start easy," I say. "Like with wine coolers."

JD shivers in disgust. After passing me a glass, he tries one last time. "You sure you don't want to give it a try? This particular bottle costs three or four thousand."

"Holy shit!" Amy exclaims. "So I've got like five hundred dollars' worth of alcohol in my glass here?"

"More like two-fifty."

Amy stares closely at her glass. "OMG."

"I'm good," Bridget says.

"Are you sure?" Amy asks her friend. "You're not in the least bit curious? I've never had anything so expensive go into my stomach before."

"I wouldn't be able to appreciate it fully."

JD continues to stare in disbelief at Bridget.

"She's good with her drink," I say.

Amy takes a sip of the *baijiu* and looks like she's ready to cry. "Holy shit."

While Amy reaches for a cup of water, JD looks at the bottle. "Guess the proof on this one is higher."

"Help yourselves to the dim sum," I tell the women.

While they collect their food, I down my *baijiu*. It's not a sipping drink. American news anchor Dan Rather supposedly said it tasted like "liquid razor blades."

A few minutes later, Amy is giggling while JD bites a dumpling off her chopsticks.

Bridget sits in a chair across from me with a small plate of food and chopsticks. "This dim sum looks amazing,"

"The forks are at the end of the table," I let her know.

She raises a brow at me. "You think that just 'cause I'm not Asian, I don't know how to use chopsticks?"

"I find most people who don't grow up using chopsticks prefer the easier utensil."

She slips the pair of sticks into her hand with ease, picks up a dumpling, and pops it into her mouth. Her eyes light up.

"Nice," I admit. "You're actually holding the sticks properly."

She swallows. "I won't say it didn't take me a ton of practice. When I was little, I went to a daycare in Chinatown. Everyone else there was Chinese except for me and one other kid. I was fascinated with chopsticks. I mean, you can't pick up a single grain of rice with any other utensil."

Chopsticks are more useful than forks in BDSM, too.

"By the way, that dumpling was...*wow*," she says.

She tries the shumai next. She chews slowly, savoring each bite. I sit and watch, slightly fascinated by her reaction. If this is how she responds to food, what does she look like when she's having an orgasm?

"Did you grow up here in the city?" I ask.

"Oakland. What about you?"

"Atherton."

"I've heard of Atherton. Isn't that the most expensive zip code in the country?"

"Off and on."

She doesn't look that impressed. The food, however, is a different story. She goes back for seconds.

"This is the most amazing dim sum I've ever had," she says after finishing a bite of the bao. A little bit of sauce clings to the corner of her mouth, and if I weren't so far away, I'd be tempted to wipe it for her.

"Though Mrs. Wang from my preschool made a mean steamed bun with ground pork," she continues. "Those buns were to *die* for."

"You like food," I observe.

"Who doesn't?"

As if in answer to her question, Kimberly appears. Kimberly is your stereotypical model who only eats lettuce.

"Eric wanted to talk to you," she explains.

As if he never saw Bridget, Eric sits on the coffee table right between us.

"You might have heard that the Drumms are thinking to bring our brand of luxury resorts to Northern California," he says.

"What about it?" I ask, annoyed that he's cut off my line of sight to Bridget. Strangely, I like watching her eat.

"We've decided to open up opportunities for partners."

"I heard Tony Lee turned you down."

Eric bristles. "That was…things got personal for Tony. Honestly, I don't know what his deal was."

Tony Lee is from a different part of the Lee family and a distant relative. He used to run with the Vietnam branch of the *Jing San* but is now trying to live on the straight and honest path. We met up at a BDSM club in Hanoi twice when I was visiting. I've invited him a few times to The Lotus, but he prefers to play at The Lair.

"You try Ben Lee?" I ask.

Eric practically rolls his eyes. "Like Tony, he's the other side of the Lee clan, right? Your side is more adventurous. You know a good business opportunity when you see it."

While Eric launches into a description of his vision for the resort, I can hear Kimberly talking to Bridget.

"Where's that sweater of yours?"

I lean to one side to look around Eric to check if Bridget is holding a drink. Bridget looks over to the sofa, where Amy and JD sit. Her sweater is draped over the arm near Amy, who has her legs on JD's lap.

"Where did you find that thing?" Kimberly.

"Goodwill," Bridget replies.

"That explains it."

"What?"

"You took it off, though. Smart move."

"I know it's not the most glamorous clothing item, but it keeps me warm."

"Oh, but it goes with the rest of you."

I shake my head. Kimberly can be a bitch for no reason. I stand up to intervene when Bridget smiles.

"Thanks," she says. "You know, I'm curious to know who did your boobs for you."

"Excuse me?"

"Don't get me wrong, they look great, just a tad overdone."

Kimberly looks ready to commit murder. Her tits are a sensitive subject. She's had them enlarged twice and prefers to pass them off as *au natural.*

She turns to Eric. "Are you ready to go?" She looks at me next. "This club isn't what it used to be."

"I'll have my assistant set up a meeting," Eric says to me as Kimberly tugs him away.

Bridget moves to the railing, her back to me.

"I'm sorry. I didn't mean to insult your ex-girlfriend," she says when I stand next to her.

"How'd you know they were fake?"

"It was a guess. She looks like she weighs a hundred pounds, but her boobs look like they weigh thirty." Leaning her arms atop the railing, she puts her head in her hands. "I'm a terrible guest."

"I probably didn't put you in the best mood. I attacked your sweater first."

"That's true, but I shouldn't have taken it out on your girlfriend."

"Ex-girlfriend. Sort-of ex-girlfriend. We weren't that committed."

I don't know why I find myself explaining this to a woman I don't expect to see again. She's raising her brows at me, too, as if I've said something wrong.

"You judging me?" I ask.

"No, I get there are gray areas in relationships."

I feel like calling her bullshit, but I spot Olga coming up the stairs. I also notice that Amy doesn't look so well.

"Darren, I've been looking for you," Olga says, coming toward me and wrapping her arm around my waist. "I feel like going up to your place. I want you to tie me up like you did to me last time."

I see Bridget raise those damn brows again.

"Olga, this is Bridget," I introduce. "Bridget, Olga."

Olga turns around, surprised that someone is there. I can tell she's inebriated by her several attempts to focus her gaze on Bridget.

"Ah…wait. Are you that ugly-sweater woman?"

I give Olga a stern look. Getting the message, she mutters a sorry and saunters over to the dim sum.

When I turn my attention back to Bridget, she looks pensive but not devastated.

"I know you guys want me to burn that sweater," she says, "but until I find something warmer, I'm keeping— Or not."

I turn around to see that Amy has upchucked all over the sweater.

CHAPTER TEN

DARREN

Present

With her wrists bound in rope, pulled loosely overhead, her ass curved outward because of the heels she's wearing, Bridget looks hot. Fucking hot.

She doesn't know it's me standing before her. She'd probably be relieved to know it wasn't strangers who had kidnapped her, though if she *truly* knew me, she'd probably be even more scared.

Why did you run out on me?

That's the burning question. But I don't ask it just yet. Instead, I run my knuckles along her arm. She flinches, and her breath shortens. I notice she has goose bumps on her arm. The basement we're in is on the cold side. I should warm it up for her, but does she deserve to be comfortable?

I graze my knuckles along her other arm. She strains away from me, and her breaths come even faster. I watch the rise and fall of her chest. I grab a breast.

From beneath the hood, I hear a groan and whimper. Her body trembles. She's scared to death.

As much as I want to punish her for leaving me and taking what's mine, I don't want her thinking a stranger is mauling her. And I don't want her so scared that she might piss herself.

I pull the hood off her head. Our gazes meet. Her eyes widen in further fright, which makes me angry. She obviously isn't pleased to see me. Her body arches away, as if it has anywhere to go.

"You think I couldn't find you, Bridge?" I ask. It's a rhetorical question because her mouth is bound with tape.

She doesn't respond. Only the sound of her breathing fills the air. She looks down. I grasp her chin to make her look at me.

"You've been a bad sub," I tell her. "Running away from your Master without a goodbye, just a fucking letter."

There's a lot of fear in her eyes. I guess it's to be expected, given that she's been kidnapped. Still, I would have thought she'd be a little relieved to know it was me instead of strangers.

I don't understand her at all. I thought I knew her. I thought she was the kind of person who was what-you-see-is-what-you-get.

But I was wrong.

She had me fooled. Played me better than fucking Manny Wu. In disgust, I release her chin roughly and turn away from her.

Maybe I should just cut her loose. If she had wanted to be with me, she wouldn't have left in the first place. She wanted to be so far from me, she moved out of state.

But, no.

She has something of mine. And I'm going to claim it.

CHAPTER ELEVEN

BRIDGET

Present

My heartbeat goes crazy. I think I'd rather be kidnapped by strangers. Maybe. Neither is good. I haven't looked into those black eyes in two years. The last time, they had seemed filled with affection. They aren't now. Shit. Is the present silence a good sign? I stare at Darren's back. He's dressed in black jeans and a t-shirt that molds his upper body. Even faced away, he looks hot.

I test my bonds again, but that gets him to turn around.

"I thought we had a good thing going, Bridge."

My heart aches. *I thought so, too, but you had to turn out to be a gangster.*

And despite the fact that he's part of a triad that's committed horrible crimes, and despite all that I've been through, I don't think all my feelings for him have disappeared. Which is crazy and stupid. So stupid.

His countenance darkens. "Guess you didn't feel the same way."

If I weren't so petrified, I'd be holding back tears. I've got to find a way out of this.

Narrowing his eyes at me, he says, "But you didn't fake all those orgasms. Did you?"

Hell no. I hadn't thought it possible for my body to experience the highs that it did with Darren.

He advances toward me till I can feel his breath on my face. He searches the depths of my eyes. "Did you?"

I shake my head.

"Prove it."

My legs weaken. What?

His gaze slices into mine. "Right here. Right now."

I stare at him, looking for evidence that he's become unhinged. Though I've never seen him be anything but collected and intentional, a lot can change in two years.

"If you can orgasm for real, I'll believe you never faked it with me," he elucidates, dashing my hopes that either he's joking or I simply heard wrong.

There's no way…!

But as my gaze drops to his lips, I'm assaulted by memories of how those lips have taken mine, how his mouth has combed the depths of mine. My body temperature ticks up.

However, what's the harm in letting him think I faked an orgasm here or there?

As if he's read my mind, he wraps his hand about my throat. "I would be so disappointed if you did. Faking an orgasm is a premeditated lie your body makes and a very punishable offense. It deserves the *severest* punishment."

He squeezes my throat, not enough to hurt but enough to spike my panic. What does he mean by the "severest punishment?" At the same time, maybe this is good news. Maybe he doesn't intend for me to suffer Amy's fate.

His hand falls from my throat and down my chest, pushing into my dress. Slipping his hand into my bra, he finds my nipple and pinches it. Hard.

I squeal. I can't pull away without making things worse for my nipple, so all I can do is stand there and take it.

"You have no idea what I'm capable of, Bridge."

I have some idea, and that's enough. I don't need to know more. I don't want to know more.

He releases my nipple, and I gasp in relief. I've got to get out of this place. The rope is bound to pipes overhead. There are no windows. I'm in a basement or warehouse.

I'm pretty sure I heard multiple footsteps before. At least three. Darren's bodyguard was probably one of them. But where were the other people? Who had his hand up my dress? And what was that gunshot I heard? Maybe it wasn't a gunshot?

Darren moves his hand back up my chest to my chin. He runs his thumb over the tape covering my lips. "So you going to come for me, Bridge? Just like you used to?"

He's serious. How am I supposed to be in the mood after I've been *kidnapped*? I've heard that adrenalin can boost arousal, so maybe I have that going in my favor.

"If I remember..." he murmurs as his fingers graze the area just past my jawbone, behind my ear.

My legs melt. That little area is an erogenous zone for me, one that he discovered. Still, given that I'm in flight-or-fight mode, I'm surprised Darren's caress can trigger a response in me.

Leaning down, he replaces his fingers. As he kisses and nibbles, I feel my mind being pulled away from the present and into the past, to a time when I would have done just about anything for Darren, when I thought he felt the same toward me.

But what a delusion that was! I was so wrapped up in my fantasy and had fallen so hard for Darren, I saw only what I wanted to see. The present is a completely different picture.

Only now I have to go back into that past fantasy and pretend like everything is okay. Otherwise, how in the world am I going to be in a state receptive to climaxing?

Gently, he licks the erogenous spot, and my body lights up. It's just like the past, like the two-plus years in between never existed.

He works the area more intensely. Part of me protests. I don't want to succumb to Darren. I don't want him thinking I still want him. I should be screaming at him, kneeing him in the balls because he kidnapped me and is holding me captive against my will.

This is what you get for falling in love with a gangster.

His hand is between my shoulder blades, slides down to the small of my back and settles on my ass. Electric pulses shoot through my body. How am I able to hold two seemingly diametrically opposed responses at the same time? Some sentimental, sex-starved part of me wants to live in the past, before I knew the truth of who Darren is. The more sensible part of me is scared, wants to put up a fight and get as far from Darren as possible.

At this point, I'm not sure which part will prevail.

CHAPTER TWELVE

DARREN

Present

I squeeze a buttock, and heat soars through me. I can sense her body responding, despite the fear swirling in her eyes. Would I continue if she didn't respond? Growing up a gangster, I don't tend toward nice. But with Bridget, I don't know. It's like some of her goodness rubbed off on me. I'm actually feeling guilty about what I'm doing to her right now.

Fuck that.

If she wanted me to be nice, she shouldn't have run out on me like she did. All that should matter is showing her that she still belongs to me. Her body is mine. If she thought she was going to give what's mine to that Ryan Gosling lookalike with the toothy grin I paid off, she has a hard lesson to learn.

With my hand on her ass, I grind her against my hard-on, silently telling her that *this* cock is the one she pledges allegiance to. Her lashes flutter quickly, and I feel myself weaken a little. I look her over. Everything about her sends my desires into overdrive. It would be so easy to just pull up her dress and drive myself into her. It's what my body wants. And what I want, I usually get.

I once talked my Asian Culture professor out of giving me the final exam. I still got an A in the class. When another member of the *Jing San* tried to open a rival club to The Lotus, I got it shut before it even opened.

Right now, I want to ravage her. I want to make up for lost time. For two plus fucking years.

I slip my hand beneath her dress. I want to feel the flesh of her ass, skin to skin. She's wearing a pair of silky bikini underpants. I remember she's not a fan of thongs because they feel like a constant wedgie to her. Which is exactly why I sometimes made her wear a pair. A constant reminder of our relationship, of her willing submission.

I flip her around and smack my pelvis into her backside. "I like how your heels make your ass stick out."

With me, she only wore heels like these if I bought them for her and commanded her to wear them. That she wore these heels for Josh upsets me. I rub her ass harder against my erection.

I push up her dress and pull down her underwear, baring her buttocks. My head swims. Her ass is fuller than I remember. I like it. I slap an ass cheek. Bridget liked spankings best. By hand, by flogger, or even a wooden paddle nearly an inch thick. With holes.

I grab an ass cheek and shake it hard before giving it another forceful slap. She grunts, but she's endured far harsher. I dig my fingers into her flesh again. Holy shit. I can't believe it's been more than two years since I had this. My cock is raging.

"Remember what it felt like to have me in your ass?" I murmur into her ear. "You think you can take it again?"

She gave me her anal cherry, but it hadn't been easy for her.

My cock has only tasted her ass twice before. And it wants more. All I have to do is take it.

Grabbing her hips, I dry hump her backside. I wonder if anyone else has gotten to experience the lushness of her ass. Had there been other Joshes? Others who had sampled what was supposed to be mine and mine alone?

It takes all my restraint not to bury myself full-hilt into her ass. I want to show her how no one can fuck her like I fuck her. I want to punish her and bring her to ecstasy at the same time.

Remembering my earlier intentions, I slow my thrusting. I want to see her orgasm. I'm not sure it'll actually prove anything, but I want her to know that she can't resist me.

I snake my right hand around her hip to her pubis. She gasps. My fingers comb through the hair there and reach lower, sliding between her folds to find her clit. At first, she strains away from touch, but after a few strokes, she relents. I rub and fondle the nub. My blood throbs to each of her shaky breaths. I scent her desire coming on. It's always the most heady aroma, more powerful and alluring than any fragrance.

My fingers dip lower and connect with wetness. I drag some of the moisture over her clit.

"That's a good start, Bridge," I say, cupping her mound fully.

Again I press my erection into her rump. With my hand still between her legs, I grope a breast with my other hand. "Remember all the fun we used to have, Bridge?"

She surrenders a soft moan. I knead the flesh of her breast through her dress and bra. Her groan quivers as my palm grazes her nipple. It's as hard as a rock. I give it a solid pinch. Her loud squeal surprises me. She was never a huge fan of nipple play, but today she seems more sensitive than usual.

Maybe it's the adrenaline.

The guilt returns, but I shove it back down. Gripping her jaw, I ask, "Remember the orgasms?"

When she doesn't respond, I give her cheek a light slap. "Remember?"

Her lashes flutter, and she nods.

I go back to caressing her clit. "I remember, too. I remember how red your ass got beneath the tawse, how you loved the suspension bondage, how wet you made my bedsheets. You always got so incredibly wet for me. The way you're wet for me right now."

I push two fingers into her cunt. The wet heat makes my head spin. For several minutes, I work her, stroking her inside, making sure to graze her clit. I can feel the tension in her body. Pulling my fingers out, I rub the moisture across the tape on her lips, below her nose for her to smell.

I squat down and take a closer look at her ass. After kissing one buttock, I jam my fingers back into her and work her good. The tension in her body seems to reach a new level, and then there's the quiet before the storm, when the quivering and the groaning stops, right before the eruption. I spread her ass cheeks with my free hand and see her anus contracting. I feel the rapid flutter of her cunt on my fingers. Even if she was doing Kegels to simulate an orgasm, she couldn't contract her pussy that fast.

Watching her climax is a high that my arousal feeds off of. I leave my fingers inside her till the last of her shudders subside, imagining it's my cock that's buried inside her. Closing my eyes, I let my desires settle before I pull away, rise, and step back.

"Nicely done, Bridge," I tell her. I pull her head back by her hair and press my mouth to her ear. "But just because you've given me a real orgasm doesn't mean you're off the hook."

CHAPTER THIRTEEN

DARREN

Past

I watch as the pretty young woman, JD's latest pussy pursuit, retches all over her friend's sweater. He takes the mojito from her hands before it starts to spill.

Bridget rushes over to her. "We should get you to the restroom."

Amy groans and slumps against the back of the sofa.

I lift a hand, and an attendant immediately appears. I glance over at the sweater, now covered in bits of chewed-up dim sum and whatever else the coed had in her stomach. The vomit drips off the sweater and onto my sofa. The attendant immediately produces a towel. Another attendant comes over with a busboy tub.

"I don't want to move," Amy mumbles.

"We should go home then," Bridget says before turning to see the attendant place her sweater into the busboy tub.

Not knowing what else to do, JD stands up. If he had expected to pound some pussy tonight, it wasn't going to happen. Behind me, Olga mutters something in Russian.

"How'd you get here?" I ask Bridget.

"BART and then taxi," she answers.

"We'll give you a lift," JD offers.

While I agree that it's not going to be easy for Bridget to maneuver Amy on and off a BART train, and perhaps not that safe for two women, one of them wasted, to take public transportation at this hour of the night, we could have just called them a cab.

JD turns to me. "Right, cuz?"

Bridget's gaze meets mine. "Oh, that won't be—"

"'Course," I answer.

She looks like she *wants* to protest further but doesn't, possibly because of the finality in my tone when I spoke. Instead, she says to the attendant wiping the sofa, "I can help with that."

"We should get your friend home," I tell her. "Besides, you're not the one who threw up all over the sofa."

"Does that matter? I'm just trying to be helpful."

"You won't be much help. That sofa's going to need to be deep-cleaned."

Or burned. Like that sweater of hers.

"Wanna take your new Panamera for a spin?" JD asks me.

I frown at him. He can't think I'm eager to chance Amy throwing up in my new wheels. I reply, "How about you have your driver bring around the Cullinan?"

"Fine, fine."

JD is more heavily involved in the *Jing San* than I am and sees a lot more money as a result. If he screwed up his ride, he could easily afford a replacement. He often pushes me to work more closely with him. My mother would rather see me sever all my ties to the triad, and it's one reason I started The Lotus. Sometimes I toy with myself, thinking that I can go completely legit. But the club wouldn't be what it is without the *Jing San*. And the *Jing San* is family.

As JD calls his driver, Bridget tries to help Amy to her feet. Amy moans. JD returns his cell to his pocket and picks up Amy. He must really want a piece of her, because he has plenty of women to fall back on for a booty call.

I sweep my arm for Bridget to go ahead and start to follow her down the stairs.

Olga puts a hand on my arm. "You are going, too?"

It's true that I don't have to tag along, but I feel almost compelled. Not sure why.

"Yeah," I answer.

She steps into me and tugs at one of the buttons on my shirt. "You coming back to the club? Or maybe I can meet you upstairs in your flat?"

"Sure."

At that, she smiles and releases the button. "Be back soon."

I head down the stairs and catch up to the others. Amy and Bridget collect their cellphones from security. Unless authorized by me, no electronics are allowed inside the club, not even watches. The policy protects the privacy of the club patrons. One of the reasons the *Jing San* is so successful is because it trusts no one.

We step outside the building into the cold night air where JD's driver is waiting with the Cullinan. Bridget gasps and wraps her bare arms around herself. I take off my jacket and put it around her shoulders.

"Thanks, but—" she starts.

But I've stepped to the vehicle to open the passenger door for myself. Bridget helps JD place Amy into the backseat and hops in after.

"Where do you live?" I ask Bridget after I tell the driver to head toward Berkeley.

"On Ever Street off Dwight Way."

The driver nods to indicate he heard.

"Thanks for the lift," Bridget says. "And if we need to cover the cost of cleaning the sofa—"

"Don't worry about it," I reply.

She doesn't press her case, and I suspect that maybe money is an issue or she would insist.

Meanwhile, JD takes a call on his cell.

"What do you mean we lost two?" he asks in Cantonese.

I'm surprised he's taking what sounds like a business call in front of strangers. Although Amy looks completely out of it, there's no guarantee that Bridget doesn't somehow know Cantonese.

"Not enough space? Better ventilation?" JD continues. "You know that's not possible. Just have Huang figure it out or the next loss is coming out of his pocket."

I look over my shoulder to see that Amy looks like she's out cold and Bridget is looking out the window. To test them, I ask, in Cantonese, if either of them speak the language.

Neither she nor Amy react.

"So what are you majoring in at Cal?" JD asks Bridget after hanging up.

"Public health," she answers.

"You want to be a doctor?"

"I'm more interested in the policy side of it. Probably get a Master's in Public Health."

"You'd make more money as a doctor."

"Sure, but I like the idea of making a difference at a community level."

JD stares blankly at Bridget, and I suppress a smile. My cousin slept through most of his classes at UCLA. He only went to college to party and meet girls.

"What did you major in?" she asks.

JD starts texting on his phone. "Asian American Studies."

"That's cool."

"Not really. But I had to pick something."

"Why'd you go to college at all?"

"Because all good Chinese boys do," he snickers. "Right, Darren?"

She raises a brow at me. "Is that true—for you, I mean?"

I had promised my mother I would go to college so that I would have something to fall back on if I chose not to continue with the *Jing San,* but I'm not sharing that with her.

Instead, I say, "It's not true...because I'm not that good."

"You're better than me," JD says. "Didn't you graduate with honors? Overachieving asshole."

"You still haven't said why you went to college," Bridget says.

I can feel her careful stare on me. "Honestly, I didn't know what else to do."

That should put an end to her questioning. To cement that, I add, "Why did you decide to go to Cal?"

"Because I wanted to further my education, and college is a pretty good place to figure out what you want to do with your life. And, sure, there's nothing like hands-on experience, but in a lot of areas, you don't want to be learning on the job. Can you imagine being hit with a pandemic and having to figure everything out as you go? It's useful to study best practices and understand the options and trade-offs beforehand."

She takes her undergraduate education a lot more seriously than I did mine.

"Shit, that's serious stuff," JD says.

Bridget turns to him. "What do you do in your import-export business?"

"Import and export goods."

"Like what?"

"Stuff you'd find boring."

"How do you know I'd find it boring?"

JD does a double take. Most women don't ask this many follow-up questions.

"*I* find it boring," he answers. "Stuff like chemical compounds."

"What are the compounds for? Pharmaceutical companies?"

"Yeah." JD looks at me for help.

I ask her, "What is your friend majoring in?"

"Amy's pre-med."

JD shakes his head. "Another addition to the stereotype."

"It's a stereotype with a small grain of truth to it," I say.

"It's got nothing to do with me."

"What, you don't like the model minority myth?"

"Fuck the model minority myth."

"At least the majority of the time, the cops don't pull you over thinking you stole the wheels you're driving, which doesn't happen for a lot of other POCs."

"That's not true. I got pulled over last week."

"Were you speeding?"

"Everyone was speeding."

"Were you driving your bright red McLaren?"

"Actually, I was driving a plain old Maserati."

"You're just a suspicious-looking son of a bitch then."

Bridget seems to have hung on our every word. She asks JD, "What's a McLaren?"

"A British car."

JD goes back to texting on his phone. A few minutes of silence passes.

"Are you guys good friends with Eric Drumm?" Bridget asks.

"You know him?" I ask.

"I know his father's running for president."

"You voting for him?"

"No."

I usually don't talk politics, but her answer was so blunt, I'm curious. "Why not?"

"As governor of Florida, he underfunded the state's public health agency, cutting the budget by half. It's one of the reasons the state was caught flat-footed with that new virus several winters ago. And he axed a school program intended to teach children about nutrition and better food choices even though the state's obesity rate hit an all-time high."

"Sounds like you should run for president."

We pass beneath a streetlight in time for me to see her cheeks color.

"I'm not old enough to," she replies.

"Would you want to if you could?"

"I don't think so. I don't have the stomach for politics."

I'm not sure I believe her. She had to have a certain thickness of skin to wear that ugly sweater of hers. Though being clueless or lacking a fashion sense might have contributed to the choice in the first place, once it became obvious how others viewed the sweater, she hadn't appeared too abashed by it.

"Why not?" I ask.

"For one, I'd have to deal with people like Eric Drumm all the time."

JD pops his head up. "What do you have against Eric Drumm? His family's a household name. They've made billions of dollars developing resorts, condos, and offices all over the world."

"I wouldn't want to work with hypocrites. They blast immigrants, but their resorts hire undocumented workers all the time."

"You can't believe everything you read in the news."

"Like how he once said he only hires women who are 'easy on the eyes?'"

"What's wrong with that?"

I silently groan. That's not the sort of response you give to someone like Bridget.

"So if a woman was smart and capable, unless she's good-looking, you won't hire her?" Bridget challenges.

"Nobody wants to admit it, but looks play a very important role. In everything. Who wants to hire an ugly-ass secretary when they can hire a pretty secretary?"

Having likely assessed JD as someone she shouldn't waste her breath on, she turns to me. "Is that how you make your hiring decisions, too?"

"You trying to pin me as sexist or misogynist?" I return.

"If the shoe fits."

This chick has some nerve. A lesson on social skills and a little time under my flogger might chill her out.

Damn. Why do I have a vision of her naked ass in my head? I don't even know what her ass looks like.

"I'm guessing you think all men are sexist," I say.

"I didn't say that."

"You're insinuating I'm sexist even though you have no evidence of how I make my hiring decisions."

"Most of the staff at your club are good-looking. Except the bouncers. They look scary, which is an asset in their job."

"So you paid attention to how my employees looked."

"I noticed, but that doesn't mean I care about how they look."

"You don't have to be defensive about it. It's biology. We can't help notice."

"I'm not being defensive."

"Do you think the patrons of The Lotus prefer to see attractive people or unattractive people serving them? I'd be a poor businessman—person—if I didn't take that into account."

"What about skills or abilities?"

"It doesn't take a lot of brains to walk around bringing drinks to people. Besides, you said looks can be assets."

"I said what?"

"When you talked about my security guys. Their appearance was an asset to their jobs."

She furrowed her brow. "Oh, right. I did."

"So appearances do matter."

"They shouldn't matter all the time."

Of course, I knew reality was more nuanced than what my statement indicated, but I was messing with her to see what her response would be. I actually agree with her assessment of Eric Drumm more than JD's and was surprised she was willing to call the guy out to someone she barely knew. That either made her opinionated or someone who speaks her mind. Or both.

I wonder what kind of submissive Bridget would make.

JD's driver pulls off the freeway, and Bridget starts giving him directions to her apartment. Eventually we pull up to a three-storied building south of campus. Mostly concrete with a brick facade, a staircase visible on the side of the structure, possibly built in the '50s, it wouldn't win any awards for attractiveness. People's Park, usually half filled with homeless tents, was two blocks away. Though I'm sure the neighborhood is hardly deemed undesirable due to its proximity to campus, compared to what I'm used to, it's ghetto.

My cell rings just as I get out of the car. It's Ronald, so I take the call.

"Dude, where are you?" Ronald asks, sounding panicked.

"Berkeley. Why?"

"What the hell are you doing there? Why aren't you at your club?"

I watch as JD and Bridget help Amy from the car. "What's the matter?"

Bridget approaches me and holds out my jacket. "Thanks for letting me borrow it."

A chilly wind kicks up just then. "Keep it," I tell her.

She balks, but I want to get back to my call. I wave her off and take a few steps away.

"Say that again?" I ask Ronald.

"Lee Hao Young is here, and he's pissed as hell that you're not here to greet him," Ronald explains. "Keeps saying how disrespectful it is."

"Hao Young finished his business and went back to his hotel."

"Well, he changed his mind and decided to come to The Lotus. Shit, man, you better get back here."

"All right, all right," I say. Hanging up with Ronald, I call Cheryl. "When did Hao Young arrive?"

"Lee Hao Young?" she asks. "He's not here."

"Are you sure? I just got a frantic call from Ronald."

"Security is supposed to notify me the instant Hao Young arrives. I wouldn't let someone as important as Lee Hao Young escape my notice."

I believe her. I hired Cheryl because of her high level of competence and trustworthiness. I could have pointed her out to Bridget as a worthy example of my hiring decisions, but I didn't feel like defending myself. It shouldn't matter what Bridget thinks of me.

"Where's Ronald?" I ask.

"Let me see… He's by the bar. Laughing his head off."

Fucking Ronald Ho.

"You want me to throw the asshole out?" Cheryl asks me.

"No. I'll deal with him when I'm back."

Hanging up, I wait by the car till JD returns.

"No coed pussy for me tonight," JD sighs as he climbs into

the car.

"Don't let her drink so much next time," I say. "She would have let you in her pants even without the alcohol."

"Yeah, yeah, but she's cute when she's drunk. I'll just invite her over to my place next time. That way she won't be bringing her dowdy chaperone with her. Talk about a turn-off."

"I don't know about that," I say, mostly to myself. What would she be like in bed? Probably not that good, but she might be coachable.

"I've met her type at UCLA," JD continues. "Feminist lesbo who refuses to accept how the world works."

"She's not off base with Eric Drumm."

"His dad's got a great chance to be fucking president of the United States. Can you imagine the strings they can pull? And you know they'll do it. Drumm's not the kind of politician who cares what the American public thinks."

"Yeah, but his dad doesn't like anything Chinese. He's worried China's going to rule the world."

"As long as there's something in it for the Drumms, that's all they care about."

I couldn't argue with that.

"If you're looking for pussy, Olga's waiting at my place," I say.

"Yeah? I could pound me some Russian cunt. But don't you want her?"

Olga would probably be willing to take us both on, but, strangely, I'm not in the mood.

86

"I've got to work something out with Ronald," I reply.

"Thanks, bro. I thought you might want to bring Olga to my sister's wedding."

JD's younger sister, Andrea, is getting married in two weeks in Phuket, Thailand.

"No," I reply. "My mom might fly over. If she does, I'll go stag."

JD wrinkles his nose. "What? You gonna make your mom your plus one?"

"She's going to bitch about whoever I bring as a date. Not sure I feel up for that. What about you? You bringing Amy?"

"Maybe. See how things go first."

As the car heads back toward the city, my thoughts bounce from Ronald to Drumm to Bridget. I remember how her body stiffened when I pulled her onto the dance floor. Why was I thinking about her so much? Because she didn't melt in my presence and make eyes at me?

By the time we make it back to The Lotus, only a dozen or so patrons remain, including Ronald, a slightly overweight guy with a square face. He's chatting up a young woman.

Seeing me, he smiles broadly. "You made it back. You missed Lee Hao Young, though."

I grab him by the back of his collar. "My office. Now."

I drag him to the office, which Cheryl also uses. Seeing me and Ronald, she jumps from the desk and exits. Marshall, who used to be my bodyguard when my dad was alive and is now head of club security, stays.

Once Cheryl closes the door, I slam Ronald down onto the desk.

"It was a joke! A joke!" Ronald exclaims.

"With a Vanguard?" I return, pushing the side of his face into the desktop.

"Can't you take a joke?" he cries.

"I'm tired of your jokes." I look up at Marshall. "Hand me your piece."

Marshall takes out his Glock and cocks it for me. I press the muzzle to Ronald's temple.

"Christ!" Ronald cries, shaking beneath me. "Okay, okay, I'll drop the jokes! I swear!"

"You think I believe you?" I snarl into his ear.

"I swear! Christ, Darren! I promise!"

"Good. Then we're even."

I back off, uncock the gun and hand it back to Marshall. Ronald, still bewildered, straightens and stares at me.

I grin. "Got you."

Marshall snickers.

"Wait," Ronald says, perplexed. "You were just…?"

"Joking," I fill in.

Looking faint, Ronald sits on the edge of the desk. "So, you weren't going to—you weren't going to kill me?"

"Not this time," I warn him.

Ronald exhales and runs a hand through his hair. "Shit. I

honestly thought...Christ. I almost pissed my pants."

"We better get you a drink."

"No shit."

Ronald gets up from the desk and we head over to the bar. I consider telling Ronald about the joke I thought he had pulled with Bridget. In retrospect, it would have been an odd joke. I shake my head and wonder if I'll ever see Bridget again. Something tells me not.

Too bad. She was kind of interesting.

CHAPTER FOURTEEN

BRIDGET

Past

As I lay in bed after setting my alarm to try and tackle statistics in the early morning, I replay the events of the night in my mind. I shouldn't have said "If the shoe fits." I probably came off judgmental to Darren. Though that's probably nothing next to the drink I threw in his face. Even though he deserved it, I start to feel sheepish. I've never done anything like that before to a stranger.

But I shouldn't worry too much about it since I'll probably never see the guy again. I *hope* I'll never the see guy again.

Or do I?

I recall how firm and strong he felt when we were on the dance floor. A part of me wouldn't have minded dancing with him longer. And even though we got off on the wrong foot, he had apologized, gave us drinks on the house and allowed us to come upstairs with him. It was nice that he didn't seem to hold the Coke-to-the-face against me. And he didn't have to give me and Amy a ride back or lend me his jacket, which I'd hung neatly in the closet because it's the most expensive thing in my possession by far. I realize I should get the jacket back to him.

Looking over at Amy, snoring in her bed, I hope this JD Lee is a good guy. I can't get a good read on him or his cousin. They're older than us, probably in their late twenties, and with their good looks and obvious wealth, they can attract just about any kind of woman. Like that uppity ex-girlfriend of Darren's.

I throw my arm over my eyes and groan. I wasn't at my best tonight. I shouldn't have let that woman get to me.

Amy snorts in her sleep, and my thoughts return to JD. I hope he doesn't view her as a cute plaything that he knows he'll get bored of sooner or later. I can see Amy falling for him, lost in the glamour that wealth affords him and his cousin. But there's more to them than that. They both have an edge I can't quite describe. A few times, I caught Darren looking at me in a way that made me think I should run and hide, yet I couldn't look away.

It was one of the stranger nights I've had, and I'm grateful when sleep finally causes thoughts of Darren Lee to fade.

*****

"You gonna make it to your Hum Bio class this morning?" I ask Amy, placing a glass of water and a bottle of pain reliever next to her bed.

She groans and covers her head with her pillow.

"There's coffee in the kitchen," I add before getting my stuff ready for the first class of the day.

"What happened?" Amy groans.

"One too many mojitos happened," I reply.

With her head still beneath the pillow, she turns onto her stomach. "Did I pass out?"

"Yeah, you did."

I hope she doesn't ask about the throwing-up part.

"*God.* I must've made such a shitty impression."

I zip up my backpack. "Well, they liked you well enough to give us a ride home."

She peeks at me from beneath the pillow. "They did?"

"Drove us all the way from the city. JD carried you to your bed."

Her brow furrows in thought. "So that's good?"

I shrug. "They didn't have to do that."

"Who's 'they?'"

"JD and his cousin."

"Did they say anything?"

"Like what?"

"I don't know. Maybe something about next time?"

I think back, but then shake my head. Amy frowns, which always makes her look younger. I almost feel like pulling out a lollipop to try to cheer her up.

"I wish I hadn't gotten so nervous," Amy bemoans. "I drink when I'm nervous. I mean, that place was so glamorous. JD and his cousin were so glamorous. And hot."

Sitting up, she reaches into her pocket for her cellphone and frowns again. I'm guessing she didn't get a text or call from JD. She lays back down. "Yeah, I'm not making it to class this morning."

I wish there was something more helpful I can say, but all I muster is, "There's enough milk left if you want cereal for breakfast."

"Where are you having lunch?"

"I made myself a sandwich. Probably going to study at Moffitt during lunch."

There are amazing eateries around campus, and relatively affordable, too, compared to other parts of the Bay Area, but eating out every day is not in my budget.

As I step out of our unit, I run into Jordan, also going down the stairs. With her designer jeans and blow-dry, she doesn't look like she's headed to class, but she's always stylish wherever she goes.

"So how was The Lotus?" she asks in a tone that reveals she's not asking because she wants to start a friendly conversation.

"Nice, I guess," I reply.

She sniffs. "Then you weren't really at The Lotus. At least not the exclusive one. Just some other club with the same name."

Whatever. I don't need Jordan's validation. "Yeah," I agree.

But this seems to irk her more. "The Lotus I'm thinking of is insane."

"I thought you've never been there."

She bristles. "It's what I've heard."

"I'm sure it's a different club anyway," I say, hoping she'll drop the subject. "The one we were at is owned by a guy named Darren Lee."

Jordan stops in her tracks, but I continue down the stairs, feeling her stare on my back.

"Darren Lee?" she echoes, catching up to me.

Darn. We *are* talking about the same club.

"You were at Darren Lee's club?" she asks incredulously.

I solve the mystery for her as to how someone like me could have been inside a place like The Lotus. "Like Amy said, she got an invite from JD Lee. Turns out he's Darren's cousin."

That seems to make some sense to her, but she's still skeptical. "Amy got the invite?"

I look at the clock on my cell. "I better run or I'll be late to class."

I jog away, leaving Jordan still a little out of sorts. I make it to statistics on time, then it's tap dancing, the one just-for-fun class I let myself have each semester. I eat my sandwich while walking to the library, where I study for two hours before my next class, Advanced Health Policy, my one afternoon class of the day. It's held in the Goldman School of Public Policy, one of my favorite buildings on the north side of campus, a quieter, more residential area.

I get there early and the previous class is still in the room, so I wait in the common area. On one of the tables, someone has left a printout of a paid summer fellowship with the State Assembly's Committee on Health Care. My eyes light up. My current internship is with a county program on food security that only lasts until the end of the semester, and it doesn't pay. A paid fellowship related to health care would be so much more up my alley than working as a barista and store clerk, the two jobs I had last summer. Grabbing my cell, I take a photo of the printout.

When I make it back to my apartment, all I want to do is hop on my computer to research the nonprofit and start putting together the application. But I run into Amy soon after I step into our room.

"Who's jacket is hanging in our closet?" she asks.

"Oh, uh, Darren," I say as I drop my backpack on the floor.

She follows me to my desk. "Why is it in our closet?"

"He let me borrow it."

"Really? How come?"

I flip open my laptop, which is on its last leg and takes forever to boot up. "It was cold last night."

"Weren't you wearing a thick sweater?"

"I was. You kinda threw up on it."

Amy's mouth drops. "I did? OMG, I am *so* sorry. Oh, shit, I can't believe I did that in front of JD and Darren! I'll pay to have your sweater dry-cleaned."

"Actually, it's probably in some dumpster back at The Lotus."

Amy grimaces. "Oh, God. I swear I will never drink that much again."

"It's okay. The sweater wasn't exactly a big hit with anyone," I recall with a wry grin as I try to get my computer to connect to the internet. That sweater did a good job keeping me warm. Now what am I going to wear in its place?

Her eyes glimmer. "You planning on returning the jacket?"

"'Course. It's not mine."

She goes to the closet and pulls out the jacket. "An excuse to go back to The Lotus."

I'm not nearly as excited as she is. She slips into the jacket, which was large on me and looks gigantic on her petite and slender frame.

"OMG, this fabric is *amazing*. Have you ever felt anything so smooth and comfy?"

Although I already know what Amy is talking about, I feel the sleeve and idly wonder how Darren's embrace compares to being wrapped in his jacket.

Holy crap. Why did that thought come into my head?

"I should text JD that we have his cousin's jacket," Amy says and cheerfully reaches for her cell.

I turn my attention to the computer and manage to get my old resume up on Google Docs. Reviewing it, I try to decide if I should update what I have or start from scratch.

"Do you think he hasn't gotten my text or he's just ignoring it?" Amy asks three minutes later.

"Maybe he's in the middle of something," I offer.

"Like what?"

"A business meeting, maybe."

"You know what he does?"

"He's…" I realize I have a pretty vague idea of what JD does for a living. "In trade or something like that. I think he said something about importing and exporting chemical compounds."

Amy makes a face. "That sounds so boring. I thought his job would be, I dunno, flashier, sexier."

I go back to working on my resume, but Amy interjects five minutes later, "People can text during business meetings."

"Maybe he put his phone on silent so he can focus."

"But it would vibrate."

"He could have lost his phone. I wouldn't worry about it."

But Amy doesn't seem placated. She scrolls through social media apps, goes to the kitchen and returns with chips, then checks her phone again.

The mother in me wants to remind her that she has a test in Human Biology that she said yesterday she needed to study hard for, but her mind is so fixed on a response from JD that it would probably be hard for her to concentrate anyway.

Nearly thirty minutes has passed since she sent her text when she finally jumps off her bed. "He texted back!"

I sigh with relief.

Amy's face lights up. "He says I can bring the jacket over to an event he's hosting tonight!"

"Cool," I reply. "Don't you have to work tonight?"

"I'll call in sick. It's at his place in the city."

"His place? I think that's a sign he's still interested in you."

"But it's an event, so there'll be other people. What are you doing tonight?"

I balk. "Study. Work on my resume."

"But it's a Thursday night. Which is the new Friday. And

Friday night is part of the weekend."

"There's this cool fellowship I just found out about."

Plus, I already went with you to the city last night, I almost added.

"His cousin might be at the event."

I bristle. "So?"

"So wouldn't it be cool if you and I hooked up with JD *and* Darren?"

"I don't need to be made fun of again."

"*Please.* I don't want to go to an event where I don't know anyone."

"You know JD."

"But he's the host. What if he has to mingle with other people? What if there are a lot of people at this event? If you go, I won't ask you for another favor ever."

"Are you even allowed to bring a friend?"

"I'll text JD, but if he says 'yes,' will you?"

I blow out my breath. "Ask Simone or Kat first. If they can't go, I'll do it."

Amy gives me a big hug. "You're the best."

Silently, I pray that one of our other roommates can make it. But I'm not so lucky. The evening rolls around and Simone, who was open to going with Amy, gets asked by her girlfriend to go to the basketball game. Kat is hanging with her new sorority sisters and hitting up some frat parties. So that leaves me. And I can't decide if the prospect that Darren might be there is a good thing or bad. Amy's suggestion that I go after Darren is ludicrous. He's not my type.

Granted, I don't know him that well. But his world of designer clothing and model girlfriends is so different from mine. Plus, he was rude to me. Wealth and good looks can make someone insensitive to those who don't have those same assets.

He did apologize and tried to make up for it, the other half of me reasons.

But I'm not sure I'm ready to completely forgive him. It's not that I'm vindictive, but something about him makes me put my guard up, like an instinct to protect myself.

CHAPTER FIFTEEN

DARREN

Present

Blood pounds in my groin as I survey Bridget in the basement of a house I'm using outside of San Francisco. The residence belongs to Old Dog, a retired triad member, and he agreed to let me use it while he's touring remote areas of the mainland. Most houses in California don't have basements, but Old Dog, a former contract killer, found them useful.

This basement doesn't have windows. A light bulb hanging from the ceiling provides incomplete lighting. But otherwise it's actually clean and tidy.

Bridget's arms stretch toward the piping she's bound to. Her skirt is hiked up over her ass, and her panties wrap her thighs just below the butt cheeks. Tied and gagged, she's mine for the taking. And my body wants to do just that. Fuck whether she wants to or not.

But a part of me holds back. A part of me wants to hear her beg for it. I've never had to force myself on a woman before. And even if I were rejected by a woman, nonconsent isn't my thing. But for better or worse, Bridget inspires emotions that aren't easy to contain. I used to think she only inspired me for the better, but now I see the flip side of that inspiration.

I caress a buttock. She releases an almost imperceptible moan. I give it a good swat, remembering all the different implements that have kissed her backside. I don't have anything on me, not even a belt I can fold in half. But seeing a sink in the corner gives me an idea.

Whipping off my shirt, I run it under the water and wring it so it's only mildly wet. I return to Bridget and see that she regards me wearily. I don't like seeing the fear in her eyes, but she shouldn't have run out on me.

Pushing aside feelings of guilt, I grasp her by the jaw. "I just gave you an orgasm, Bridge. Where's my thank you?"

She stares at me, making me feel like a fucking demon, before mumbling something. Maybe a thank you. I decide not to give a shit.

"You know the rules," I tell her. "Forgetting to thank your Master is grounds for punishment."

She speaks more forcefully, but the tape muffles her words.

Walking behind her, I slap the shirt against her ass. She grunts. I smack her harder. She yelps.

I whip the shirt against her bare thighs several times, then flip the shirt over my shoulder as I bend down to untie her ankles. Standing back up, I nudge her feet apart.

"Wider," I command.

She hesitates for a moment before spreading her legs.

Grabbing the shirt, I slice it between her legs. She cries out into her gag.

I want to snap the damp shirt against her breasts, too, but I don't want to untie her to take off her dress just yet. So I whip her breasts through her clothes. Then I land the shirt on her ass, first the right cheek, then the left, then right again. I pause to feel her between the thighs. She's more wet than the last time I checked. I press two fingers up into her wet heat. Fuck, that feels amazing. I work my digits inside her for a few short minutes before withdrawing.

I backhand the shirt on her ass again, which is blushing nicely. I should spank her till she can't sit for days, and I may do just that, but my hard-on is raging seeing her ass turn crimson for me.

Stemming my ardor, I whip the shirt against her pussy, her legs, and back to her ass again. She squirms. Her body instinctively wants to avoid the brunt of the blows, but she knows better than to eschew her punishment. She knows that doing so will worsen her consequences.

Whap! Whap!

The shirt snaps against her ass as loud and as cutting as the tawse. I can't hold out much longer. I haven't tasted that pussy in over two years. She could do better offering water to a man who's been stranded in the desert for weeks than deny me access to her body.

I hang the shirt over my shoulder and, standing beside her, reach between her legs again, caressing her clit. A tremor goes through her. Her breath is uneven from all her grunting and cries. I fondle her swollen bud. In a more patient state, I would relish every whimper, every groan. But the tightness in my crotch is unbearable.

I sink my fingers into her again. "Were you planning on giving this to Josh?"

She doesn't look at me.

"Did you forget that this is mine?" I growl, pushing my fingers in deeper, fucking her more vigorously.

Her lashes flutter quickly.

Pulling my fingers out, I grab her jaw and force her gaze to mine. "Did you?"

I can't tell for sure, but it seems like desire mixes with fear in her eyes. She mumbles something against the tape. I remove it, freeing her mouth. She looks at me with pleading eyes.

I'm sorry, I expect her to say. *I was wrong to leave you. I'm yours. I won't ever run from you again.*

At least that's what I wanted to hear.

Instead, she says,

"Fuck me."

CHAPTER SIXTEEN

BRIDGET

Past

"**O**MG."

Both mine and Amy's jaws drop as the driver Amy booked using a ride-hailing app pulled up in front of a mansion with gabled roofs and the largest windows I have ever seen.

"Damn," the driver whistled. "You ladies must be going to some party."

"I can't believe he lives here," Amy whispered, her eyes wide with awe.

Dressed in a black halter dress she bought just for the occasion, Amy pulls out her cell and snaps a photo of JD's house. I adjust the white crepe jumpsuit I borrowed from Simone. It's a little tall on me, as I have to shop the petite section in stores, and necessitates wearing high-heels so the bottoms of the pant legs don't drag on the floor. The shoes I borrowed from Kat run small on me, and heels and I don't get along for the most part.

Wearing clothes that aren't mine and having let Amy do my hair and makeup, I feel like an imposter. At least I probably look the best I've ever looked since prom.

Two valets opens the car doors for us. I grab Darren's jacket and drape it over my arm. We step out of the car and stand beneath soft golden lanterns hanging from the archway above the entry. A beautifully dressed hostess greets us, takes our names, checks her tablet, and tells us the reception is being held on the back balcony.

In the foyer stands a young man with a tray of champagne flutes.

"Just one," Amy tells me. "I bet it's really expensive champagne."

"It's an Armand de Brignac," the server tells us.

Amy turns to me. "See?"

I'm willing to bet Amy has never heard of Armand de Brignac. I certainly haven't.

After Amy takes a glass, the server presents the tray to me, but I shake my head. Seeing a woman manning the coat check, I decide to have her hang up Darren's jacket. She takes the jacket and tells us to head down the hall, which will take us to the balcony.

We walk on gleaming stone flooring, past Asian-themed art and windows draped with stylish window treatments.

"This house is gorgeous," Amy says as we approach an expansive living area with wall-to-wall glass doors leading to the balcony, which was already filled with guests.

"I've never been in a more amazing house," I agree as I nearly trip over a rug. I fear I'm going to have to spend most of the time sitting down. These heels are not my friend.

Right before we make it outside, a server offers us a selection of appetizers: puff pastries with some kind of pâté, caviar and smoked salmon canapés, and lobster salsa with guacamole on top of a mini fried wonton wrapper.

"OMG, all this looks sooooo good," Amy drawls.

I help myself to the lobster appetizer, but Amy doesn't partake.

"Miss?" the server asks her.

"No thanks," Amy replies. She turns to me. "I don't want to get anything stuck in my teeth."

"I'd do a teeth check for you," I assure her before taking a bite of my appetizer. *Oh, man, she is missing out.*

"But what if I can't get it out?"

We step outside, which would have been chilly to say the least if not for the outdoor heat lamps. Garlands of string lights glow softly overhead. I gasp at the view of the bay and Golden Gate Bridge. Across the water, the lights of Marin County twinkle back at us.

Amy and I hang back for a moment. We're probably among the youngest event attendees. We know no one.

"I can't believe JD's asking at least two thousand per guest for Drumm," a man says to another as they walk past us to enter the house. "That's almost the max for the primaries."

I spot a blond wearing a low-cut dress standing beside a table with remit envelopes. A middle-aged man with a receding hairline flirts with her and eventually takes out his checkbook.

"Is this a fundraising event for Drumm?" I ask Amy.

Amy shrugs. "Have you seen JD yet?"

An older man comes up to Amy. "You're Jerry Chou's kid, right?"

"Actually, my name's Amy Liu. I'm a friend of JD's."

Taking a step closer, the man ogles Amy. "Are you sure you're not Aileen Chou?"

"Speaking of JD, we'd better find him," I say to Amy. Taking her by the arm, I lead her away.

"Thanks," Amy says when we're in the clear. "That man was so close I could smell the alcohol on his breath."

A server stops by with appetizers served in shot glasses, and tiny spoons.

"You sure you don't want to try the food?" I ask Amy, helping myself to a glass of what looks to be minced shrimp with avocado and mango.

Amy shakes her head.

"Wow," I say after taking a bite. For me, the food is definitely going to be the best part of the night.

As I finish the ceviche, Amy and I stand around a bit, still looking for JD. I see Eric Drumm schmoozing with the guests and wonder if Darren's ex-girlfriend is also here.

She is, and with my luck, she spots us and heads in our direction. I groan softly.

"Who is she again?" Amy whispers to me.

"Darren's ex, but I think she's Eric's girlfriend now," I reply and brace myself.

"You're not wearing a sweater tonight," Kimberly says to me.

Because I didn't have one ugly enough for the occasion.

Instead, I only smile. At The Lotus, I wasn't my best with Kimberly, and I want to be better this time. Coretta, a neighbor who helped look after me while my grandmother worked, would voice the old adage that if you can't say something nice, say nothing at all.

"Love the dress," Amy says genuinely to Kimberly.

The dress is incredibly sexy with its spaghetti straps, cowl decolletage and shimmery fabric. But the compliment doesn't really land.

"Your outfits are…nice," Kimberly returns.

Amy furrows her brow, unsure if Kimberly is returning the compliment or doing the opposite. I know exactly what Kimberly means and just keep on smiling.

"Hey! You made it!"

It's JD. And Darren.

Seeing them approach, Kimberly decides to move on.

JD smiles at Amy. "You look great."

"Thanks. So do you," Amy replies.

JD turns to me. "Barbara, right?"

"Bridget," Darren supplies.

Maybe it's the lighting, but he looks even more suave than I remember. His hair is gelled back, and he wears a sports jacket over slacks and a button-up shirt. His gaze feels like it takes in all of me. I don't know why I care, but suddenly I have Amy's food concern and hope I don't have anything caught in my teeth.

"Right. Bridget," JD says. "You girls want anything to drink?"

"Um, sure," Amy answers. "That champagne tasted good."

I opt for water. JD waves a server over and places the drink order.

"Your jacket is with coat check," I say to Darren.

"Thanks for bringing it," he replies.

"JD, your house is so frickin' amazing," Amy says.

"I can give you a quick tour," JD replies. He turns to his cousin. "Be right back."

Darren and I look at each other while JD leads Amy away. The mischievous part of me wants to ask if I get a tour, too, but I know they'll be glad for their time alone.

Remembering the coat check ticket, I fish it out of my purse and hand it to him. "Thanks again for letting me borrow your jacket. I'm a wuss when it comes to chilly weather. I think my ancestors must have lived near the equator."

The server returns with my drink and Amy's.

"Guess I'll hold on to hers," I say.

Darren waves off the server and Amy's drink. "We'll get another glass for her when she comes back."

I take a sip of my water and contemplate for a moment before saying, "It's a good vintage."

The statement's a bit corny, but he might be a tiny bit amused.

Looking for small talk, I say, "This house *is* amazing. This view is to die for."

"It's even more amazing from the gazebo, where the trees aren't in your way."

Spotting the gazebo he's referring to, I perk up.

"Let's go," Darren says.

Though his tone isn't overtly bossy, I notice he didn't *ask* if I wanted to go check out the gazebo. He must have noticed my interest.

"Sure," I say, as if he did ask.

He gives me a brief glance. I can't tell if it's quizzical or amused or weirded out. He nods in the direction of the stairs at the end of the deck.

It's not easy going down stairs in the heels I've got, and despite my best efforts, I stumble just before we reach the bottom. Darren catches me by the arm. A subtle shiver goes through me.

"Thanks," I mutter.

We make our way down a lighted path to the gazebo. I feel my ankles wobble a few times, but I manage to stay upright. There are two steps up into the gazebo, and Darren holds out an arm as if ready to catch me if I fall. Once I make it into the gazebo, I sigh at the vista. I've never seen anything more picturesque.

"I love the reflection of the lights in the water," I remark. "And the Golden Gate must be like the most beautiful bridge in the world."

"There's the Charles Bridge in Prague, the Ponte Vechhio, or Chengyang in China...but, yeah, the Golden Gate tops my list."

Without heat lamps, the gazebo is cold, but I don't want to part with the view just yet.

"You've seen these other bridges?" I ask.

"I did a semester in Italy when I was at UCLA and did some traveling then. And I've been to China a number of times."

"Do you have family there?"

"Distant relatives."

"Do your parents live here in the Bay Area?"

"My mom spends most of her time in Singapore these days. My dad passed away a few years ago."

There's a grim set to his jaw, so I decide not to ask about his dad.

We stare at the view in silence till he asks, "What about your parents?"

"My father died while on active duty before I was even born. He didn't even know about me. Took my grandmother completely by surprise when my mom dropped this baby off with her. My mom's off in Europe somewhere now. I was raised by my paternal grandmother. And her best friend and neighbor, whom I call Aunt Coretta even though she's not related."

Darren regards me. "Where does your grandmother live?"

"Oh, she passed two years ago from breast cancer."

"I'm sorry to hear."

I look at him closely. It's hard to tell if he's sincere or just playing the part of the polite babysitter, a role his cousin deftly left him in.

"She was an amazing woman," I continue. "She did so much for me. I only wish I could have done something special for

111

her, like take her on a dinner cruise around the bay or give her a spa day. She always wanted me to save whatever I earned for college."

"She sounds practical. College is expensive."

"For you, too?" I couldn't help asking.

"I guess 'expensive' is a relative term."

I go back to admiring the view. "This is so beautiful, I could stare at this for hours. I guess if importing and exporting chemical compounds can buy a view like this, I shouldn't rule it out."

Darren doesn't say anything. I rub my arms to warm them.

"Is this event a fundraiser for Drumm?" I ask.

"Yes."

"Are you supporting Drumm?"

"I'm supporting my cousin."

"But not Drumm?"

He narrows his eyes. "What does it matter?"

"Just curious to know where your politics land."

"I don't have any politics."

I frown. "Don't you vote?"

"Sometimes."

"Then you have some 'politics.' It's not a bad thing. People talk about it like it's some disease, but really, it just means you have beliefs."

"And if I did support Drumm?"

I shrug. "You have a right to."

"You wouldn't try and talk me out of it?"

"Can I?"

"No. I don't want to talk about Drumm. Like I said, I'm here to support JD."

"Is it true people had to pay two thousand dollars to attend tonight?"

"Something like that."

I look and count at least three dozen people. "So Drumm will have raised over fifty thousand dollars tonight? That amount of money could feed so man hungry families."

"I can see where *your* politics land."

I lift my chin. "Good. It's not like I'm trying to hide it."

"In my world, it's best to be…open-minded about politics."

In his world? The world of business or club owners?

A breeze kicks up, and I rub my arms more. Darren takes off his sportscoat and hands it to me.

"We could just go back inside," I demur.

"You like the view. Take it."

"Won't you get cold?"

I quiver, but it's only partially due to the cold. Mostly it's the look he's giving me. Like I'm about to be punished.

"No," he answers.

I hesitate, then take his jacket and slip it on. I catch the faint smell of him on the jacket.

"Thanks," I say. "For someone I thought was the rudest guy I'd ever met, you're actually kind of nice."

Shoot. I regret the words as soon as they leave my mouth. I didn't mean to make a backhanded compliment. Something about him makes me get my circuits crossed. And there's that look he's giving me again. Letting me know I'm in trouble.

CHAPTER SEVENTEEN

DARREN

Past

Part of me wants to demand she give me my fucking sportscoat back. The other part of me wants to pin her against the gazebo and…

I shake off the thought and decide to be nice about it. "That supposed to be a compliment?"

"I'm sorry. That came out all wrong. I mean, I did think you were rude when we first met—"

"I thought we were even once you threw your drink all over me."

"Yeah." She gives me a smile. "We're even."

Turning back to the view, she seems to soak it in as if savoring every drop of a fine wine. Maybe it's because I've seen this view many times before, but I don't remember it being this spectacular.

"Can you imagine waking up to this every day?" she asks, leaning against the guardrail. "I grew up in the flats of Oakland, and there aren't views like this."

At present, I'm more intrigued with her reaction than the view.

"You live in Oakland all your life?" I ask.

"Yep. Went to a preschool in Chinatown and graduated from Oakland Tech."

"And you said your grandmother raised you?"

"With a lot of help from Aunt Coretta, who's like a second mom to me. Aunt Coretta worked part time and took care of me after school."

"What did your grandmother do?"

"Worked for the US post office. Worked up until she had to get treatment for breast cancer, got chemo, then went back to work as soon as she could."

"Did the chemo work?"

"No. The cancer came back, and she wasn't up for going through it a second time."

My conversations with women rarely end up in territory like this, especially when I barely know them. But it almost feels natural talking to Bridget about anything.

"I had an uncle who died of lung cancer," I share. "We knew it was coming because he smoked twenty-four seven. He would eat and drink with a cigarette in his mouth. But it's tough to watch a loved one die a slow death."

I also think of Henry Fong, a fellow triad member who had to watch his father bleed to death from a single gunshot wound. The father had tried to embezzle funds, a little here, a little there, thinking he could escape detection. My mother played mahjong with Henry's mother, and she started pushing me in a different direction after what happened to Mr. Fong.

"My grandmother got really sick when I was five years old,"

Bridget says while shifting her gaze up to the sky. "She thought she might die and told me that if she passed, she would be watching me from that star there."

I follow her gaze. "That specific star?" I ask.

"The brightest one. Maybe that's the one your dad's on, too."

I'm not five years old. I feel myself resisting her comforting attempt. It's corny. I don't need it. Gangsters don't get to hang out in the heavens on stars.

But it would be cool if he were.

"What was your dad like?" she asks.

Why does she want to know that? It's an innocent enough question, I guess, but kind of intimate for two people who are hanging out together only because we got ditched by JD and Amy. Although…I'm not in a hurry for my cousin to come back.

"A quiet man. Worked a lot."

"What did he do?"

"He was a businessman."

"What kind of business?"

I can't decide if she's being conversational or just plain nosy. I wonder how she'd do if we had a session in which she could only talk if I give her permission. That might be kinda fun. Or maybe I'd help her out by stuffing a ball gag in her mouth.

"International," I reply.

"International business doing what?"

Definitely a gag. I have a muzzle, too, that covers the whole lower face, but she'd look prettier in a ball gag.

"Why are you that interested?" I throw back at her, even though talking about business is pretty harmless. I don't, however, want her to ask about how he died. Of course, I would make shit up instead of telling her the truth, that he was killed by a fellow inmate while serving time at the United States Penitentiary in Victorville.

She seems a little taken aback. "I'm sorry. We can talk about something else."

Shit. I probably came off defensive.

"My dad wasn't around a lot because of his job," I explain, "so it's not my favorite topic."

That kind of emotional stuff always has an impact on women. Sure enough, Bridget gives me a look of understanding.

"So what do you want to talk about?" she asks.

Whether you would be up for trying a spider gag instead of a ball gag.

Fuck me. I need a play session more badly than I thought.

"Do we have to talk about anything?" I return.

"No, we don't. I guess I take after my grandmother. She liked to talk. So maybe it would work out, her being on the same star with your dad."

I give a short chuckle at the idea of her grandmother talking my dad's ear off. But being quiet for my dad was a strategy for learning more about his opponents and people he had to deal with.

She goes back to falling in love with the view and seems perfectly fine with the silence between us. All the women I know would think something was wrong if a man didn't talk.

To my surprise, I'm the one breaking the silence. "You like it at Cal?"

She perks up. "Of course! What's not to like? It's a great campus, it has professors who are world leaders in their fields, there's such a rich history to the school. I mean, I wish I could get all the classes I wanted and that it cost a lot less, but I feel lucky to be there. What about you? Did you like LA?"

"It was okay," I reply.

"Just okay?"

"I don't think I'm much of a college-going guy, so it probably wouldn't have mattered where I went."

Glancing back at the party, I spot my cousin and Amy. "Looks like JD's done giving the tour."

"Guess we should head back then."

I watch her take careful steps down from the gazebo and walk awkwardly across the stone path.

"Something wrong with your shoes?" I ask.

"Ugh, they're not mine," she answers. "I'd have to be a masochist to buy shoes like these."

I'm intrigued. "Yeah? So you're not a masochist?"

She gives me a look that tells me how strange she finds my question. "You know a lot of masochists?"

"A fair number. I know a lot of women who wear shoes like yours."

"Maybe they have iron feet and are impenetrable to pain."

Which reminds me that I haven't played with bastinado in a while. I say, "Actually, parts of the feet are very sensitive to pain."

"I believe it."

When we make it back to the stairs to the deck, I look up to see Kimberly staring down at us. Bridget sees her, too, and remembers she's wearing my jacket.

She takes it off and hands it to me. "Thanks."

My hand grazes hers as I take the jacket from her. I can tell she noticed.

"I'm going to find the bathroom," she says. "Can you let Amy know?"

"Take the hall back toward the entrance. Bathroom's on your right," I tell her.

Kimberly comes up to me after Bridget's left. "Wow, you're slumming it these days. At least she's wearing something halfway decent, though she probably got her outfit from some discount store."

She's got the wrong idea about me and Bridget, but instead of refuting her assumption, I reply, "Like you're doing any better with Mr. Three Inches?"

She scowls. "How would you know what the length of his dick is?"

"You know what his father's like. A man who needs to pump himself up the way he does has size issues below the belt, and the apple doesn't fall far from the tree."

"Well, you're wrong. He's not three inches."

"Good for you."

I don't really give a fuck about Eric's dick size, but since

Bridget wasn't here to defend herself, I thought I'd do it for her. I stand close to Kimberly.

"He could be thirteen inches long," I murmur into her ear. "He still can't get you to come like I can."

Her lips are parted, her breath uneven. Leaving her in that state, I step back and walk over to my cousin.

"Bridget went to the bathroom," I inform Amy.

Amy looks me over. "Looks like you made it through without getting a drink all over you."

JD laughs. "I wish I could have been there. Where'd you find her?"

"Bridget? We met in English class as freshmen. I like her."

"Hey, I'm not knockin' her. She's just not as cool as you."

Amy blushes. "I'm gonna make sure Bridget found the bathroom okay."

The bathroom's not hard to find, but I don't say anything.

"Thanks for taking one for the team," JD says to me when Amy's gone.

"What do you mean?"

"Keeping that Bridget girl company."

"It was nothing. And I got the bonus of making Kimberly jealous."

JD raises his brows. "No joke? Kimberly was jealous of Amy's friend?"

"Why not?"

"I dunno. She's just…"

"Different," I say, wondering what Bridget would be like in bed.

"Bro, you're not seriously interested?"

I look through the glass doors and see Amy and Bridget returning. Maybe it's because I'm bored, but my answer to JD is a yes.

*****

Kimberly's pissed at me. I can tell by the way she stares and frowns at me, her passive-aggressive way of telling me I need to ask her what's wrong and make amends. She's so busy being angry at me, she hasn't picked on Bridget so far.

"You've got to try big game hunting," Eric is saying to JD as we stand on the deck after the event has wound down. "Five years ago, my dad and I got to accompany the president on his visit with the leader of Mongolia. I shot myself an argali sheep. It was so awesome!"

Bridget frowns. "You get a thrill shooting defenseless animals?"

"They're not defenseless. Have you seen their horns?"

"I assume you fired from a safe distance away."

"That's only 'cause the Nosler M48 gives you amazing range."

"Aren't argali sheep on the endangered species list?"

Eric bristles.

Not backing down, Bridget continues, "And did the taxpayers end up paying for this hunting trip?"

Everyone around us looks too stunned and uncomfortable for words. I'm kind of amused.

JD tries to come to Eric's defense. "Are you one of those please-don't-shoot-Bambi anti-hunters?"

"I didn't know 'anti-hunters' was a thing," Bridget replies, "but if you're asking if I'm someone who opposes killing endangered animals on the taxpayer's dime, then yes, I am."

Amy gives Bridget a *please stop* look.

Kimberly wakes from her coma of anger and redirects toward Bridget. "But you're in support of wearing sweaters that look like dead animals?"

Bridget gives Kimberly an *oh, please* look and opens her mouth.

But I take her by the elbow. "I forgot to show you the view from the kitchen."

She stumbles a little as I pull her into the house. "Really?"

"I could ask the same to you," I reply, not releasing her until we're in the kitchen.

"I was just speaking my mind. Men get praised all the time for straight-talking, but when women do it, we're considered bitchy."

"Did I say you were being a bitch?"

She pouted her lips for a second, reminding me of a second cousin's nine-year-old daughter, but then Bridget lifts her chin and crosses her arms. "Why'd you drag me in here then?"

"For multiple reasons, one of them being that you and Kimberly looked like you were about to tear each other's hair out."

"She started it."

"Yeah, she did, but you can still be the mature one."

I can't believe the words coming out of my mouth. I sound like my mother.

"That's exactly what I was going to tell your ex!" Bridget says. "She needs to grow up. Besides, I would never get into a physical altercation with another woman unless it was self-defense."

I'm not so sure about that. I'm sure she *believes* what she says, but the woman did throw Coke in my face. I imagine her and Kimberly going at it. That would be something sexy to bet on.

"So now that we've cleared that up…" she says, turning to head back.

My arm shoots out toward the refrigerator, blocking her path. "We're not done."

Surprised, she doesn't say anything and only looks at me. I realize I'm standing really close to her, my body inches from hers.

"You going to play nice when we get back?" I ask her.

She scrunches her face. "I'm just calling Eric out on some of the things he does. He's a politician. He should be able to take it."

"Look, I'm not a fan of Drumm, but this is an event my cousin is hosting for him. I want it to go well for JD."

She draws in a breath and leans her back against the black stainless-steel door of the refrigerator. Her lips are within kissing distance, and I wonder what her mouth tastes like, feels like.

Looking up at me, she apologizes. "I'm sorry…"

I stare at her lips.

Do it. Kiss her.

What am I scared of? That she'll accuse me of sexual assault? But I think she wants it, too. I can feel it in the vibes coming off her body.

I lower my head, fully expecting a palm to the side of my face.

But a server walks in to set down an empty tray on the kitchen island. Bridget takes the opportunity to slip away.

"I'll be good," she tells me.

You'd better, or I'll have to bring out my paddle.

Goddamn. I have something to get out of my system.

We head back to the deck and bump into Eric and Kimberly, who look like they're leaving.

"We still gotta talk about the resort project," Eric tells me. "JD says he wants in. I really appreciate this fundraiser, by the way. Raised sixty-five thousand. Not bad."

I expect a snarky comment from Bridget to follow, but she stays quiet.

"I'll have my secretary call yours," Eric says as he and Kimberly head out.

Having changed her tactic to one where she completely ignores Bridget's existence, Kimberly says, "Bye, Darren."

When we make it back to the deck, no one is left but two servers who are cleaning up. We look around briefly before going back inside. In the living room, Bridget plops down on a sofa and takes off a shoe.

"My feet are killing me. Where do you think JD and Amy went?" she asks as she rubs her foot.

"My guess? Upstairs," I answer.

Catching on to what I'd insinuated, Bridget returns an "oh." She removes her other shoe and grimaces.

"Here," I say, sitting as I take her foot and start to massage it.

Her mouth opens, probably to object, but she says nothing as I rub away the tension.

After a few minutes, Bridget sinks into the sofa, turning to lean her back against the armrest and allowing me to pull her feet onto my lap. "Wow. Did you get a minor in massage while at UCLA?"

"It's been a while, but I had a lot of practice with foot reflexology on a trip to Bali."

I don't add that it was with Kimberly.

"How long were you in Bali, and is it as magnificent as its reputation?"

"Just over two weeks, and it's pretty sweet, but everyone has their own take."

"What was the best part about Bali? The beaches?"

After applying pressure to the area of her ankle and toes, I work her heel.

"Mmmm," she murmurs.

She seems to have forgotten her question. Her eyes have closed. In silence, I continue the massage, running my knuckle along the arch of her foot, then walking my thumb along the spine of one foot, then the other. Her body is responsive. I can sense the relaxation in her.

"Want me to continue?" I ask.

"Mmhmm," she exhales.

I move to the area above her heel, the area connected to the pelvic region. Her eyes remain closed but her eyebrows lift. After a few minutes, I move to her big toe. Her bottom lip drops and her brow furrows. She looks like she's in deep concentration.

I know that look. Seen it dozens of times just before a woman orgasms.

Abruptly, Bridget closes her mouth. Eyes open, she sits up, pulling her feet from me. She appears confused and dismayed.

"You want me to finish the massage?" I offer, leaving out, *so you can get to the climax.*

"I'm good," she says. After being deeply relaxed, she's now in the opposite state, her breath uneven.

I'm disappointed because I want to know what she looks like when she orgasms. The area about my own pelvis is churning with energy.

Avoiding my gaze, she tucks a strand of hair behind her ear. Like her, I don't move or say anything for a moment. I hadn't intended for the foot massage to become sexual. Not everyone responds that way to reflexology. Kimberly didn't climax from foot massages, but she did say the sex we'd had after a couples massage session was the best she'd ever had.

"I'm going to help myself to a glass of water from the kitchen," Bridget says, getting off the sofa. "You want anything?"

I eye her closely. *Coward.*

I'm going to need something stronger than water to take the

edge off the hardness in my pants.

"There's a bar right here," I say, getting up and walking over to get her a glass of water.

She drinks the whole glass. "Thanks. Should we help clean up?"

I stare at her. That's what the hired help is for. Is she that bored or disconcerted with my company that she wants to pick up garbage?

But I surprise myself when the word that falls from my mouth is "sure."

I need my head examined. And JD owes me for this.

CHAPTER EIGHTEEN

BRIDGET

Present

His nostrils flare. He looks livid. And ravenous.

My ass is on fire from the walloping Darren gave me with his damp shirt, but the area between my legs is also a hot mess. I don't understand how I can be so turned on despite the fear still coursing strongly through me. I can't help but run my gaze over his chiseled chest and six-pack. He looks as good as ever, his body covered in a gorgeous golden tan. Physically, he's perfect. And maybe some primal, animalistic part of me, one that's not synced mentally, is drawn to his masculinity and even the way he dominates me. It's the part that's living in the past, of what we used to be, or what I thought we were, rather.

But I have another reason for telling him to fuck me. I don't know what he has planned, and I'm too afraid to ask. If I ask, and he tells me the truth, he might have to go through with it. Whatever he intends, it's best I stall him and see if I can get on his good side.

His fingers dig into me as he grips my jaw, but I manage to say again, "Fuck me."

His grip tightens. "You sure you want that, Bridge?"

"Please. No one makes me come like you do."

He seems to doubt me. "Yeah?"

I said what I did to flatter him, but it's also true. I haven't had sex with that many guys, but none of them came close to what Darren does to me. I lower my gaze as I recall some of the most mind-blowing orgasms I have ever experienced.

"And how do you want to be fucked?" he asks.

Oh boy. I feel like I've done just about everything, every position with Darren. I've even let him in my backdoor, which had been, to my great surprise, amazing. But it's been over two years, and I'm not sure I can take it there. Darren likes anal sex, though.

"However you want…sir," I reply.

With a growl, he releases me. He undoes his jeans and yanks them past his hips. His cock springs up. My breath catches. I haven't seen a man's cock in over two years, and never thought I'd see this particular one ever again.

He strokes himself. "This what you want, Bridge?"

Warmth surges in my groin as I stare at what I consider to be a perfect erection. "Yes, please."

"Do bad subs deserve cock?"

Feeling the emptiness between my legs, I whimper. Meeting his gaze, I say, "You could punish me with it."

His countenance is grim as he returns my stare. "I should. Punish you. Use you like my fucktoy. That's all you're good for, right?"

Ouch. Maybe he's just thinking out loud. Maybe he wants to be mean. Either way, it hurts.

"Yes, sir," I reply, lowering my eyes.

He fists his hand in my hair and yanks my head back, making me look at him. "Is that what you want to be? My fucktoy?"

Overdue anger starts to stir in me. "It doesn't seem like I have a choice, do I?"

With a snicker, he releases my hair. I'm glad because it stung. Why are there so many nerves on the scalp, anyway?

He goes back to stroking his cock. "If I told you to suck me off, would you do it?"

"I loved sucking your cock," I remind him.

"Did you miss it?"

"Yes."

"Bullshit."

"I missed your cock," I assure him.

"Where did you miss it the most? Your ass?"

I falter. "My…my pussy."

"My cock missed your pussy, too. And your mouth. But it missed your ass most of all."

I take a breath and brace myself for anal sex. I hope he has lubricant.

He jerks himself a little more forcefully while pondering aloud, "Which hole to take first?"

If he wants a blow job, he'll have to undo or loosen the ropes that are holding me up.

"I could suck you off good," I tell him. "Remember how good I got?"

He frowns. His jaw tightens. I've said something wrong, maybe.

"You made a lot of progress," he agrees. "A real 'A' student. Don't worry. You'll get a chance to blow me. I just don't feel like untying you right now."

Damn. How am I going to get myself free? How long is he going to just play with me? Not that I want to be his toy forever, but it's better than what he might intend after he's done fucking around with me.

Cock in hand, he walks around to my backside. He gropes a buttock. "I missed this ass of mine, so maybe I'll take the backdoor first."

"I don't have any lube on me," I signal.

"Sure you do."

His hand reaches beneath my butt and rubs the moisture between my thighs. He inserts two, then three fingers into me. For anal sex, I usually have to feel pretty raunchy and horny. I'm not quite there yet, but it's looking like I don't have a choice. Coming usually puts Darren in a more open and affectionate mood, and if he has any feelings for me left, I need to tap into them.

Although, there is a chance that once he's come, he'll have no use for me anymore. He will have punished me, used me, and the next thing would be to dispose of me…

He pulls his fingers out and circles one of them about my back opening. My breasts tingle. Maybe I can work myself up for this.

Closing my eyes, I recall the first time I orgasmed with anal penetration. It had blown my mind that such a thing could happen. That made me a convert, such that I looked forward to anal sex. But we had worked up to it. The first time Darren sank his cock into me had hurt. Was it going to be like that all over again?

"Anyone or anything been back here since you've been gone?" he asks.

"No," I answer firmly.

"Should I believe you?"

"Why would I lie?"

He presses a digit past my sphincter. "I don't know, Bridge. You ever lie to me before?"

I swallow a grunt as my body resists the intrusion. It's going to be like the first time. Damn.

I shake my head and lie, "No."

He sinks his digit deeper. "Fuck, you're tight. Guess you might be telling the truth on that one."

Slowly withdrawing his finger, he inserts a different finger. My anus pushes against the intrusion. I take several calming breaths. It doesn't matter if I'm going to like the anal sex or not. I just need *him* to like it. A lot. Maybe then he'll want to keep me as his fucktoy, buying me more time to figure out how to escape.

"You're going to need more lube," he considers aloud as he pulls out his finger. He grabs a buttock and, with his other hand, he guides his shaft to my slit.

Pleasure flutters through me as his tip pushes against me. My body remembers this, remembers all the rapture. He sinks himself farther. Oh God, yes. Not having had sex in over two years didn't seem like that big a deal between the pregnancy and living in fear for nearly a year before I finally wasn't looking over my shoulder every other minute. Then, between the broken sleep, the challenges of breastfeeding, and the schoolwork, sex just wasn't a priority.

But now I recall what I missed. And not just sex itself. Sex with Darren.

With both hands on my hips, he pulls me back onto his cock as far as I can go. And it feels frickin' fantastic. My pussy grabs onto him like it won't let go.

"Your pussy missed my cock, didn't it?" Darren murmurs.

"Yes."

"Has it gotten a good pounding lately?"

"No."

"Does it want one?"

I hesitate, remembering how hard Darren can fuck. But I can't refuse.

"Yes, please," I answer quietly.

"Your pussy is always up for a good pounding, isn't it?"

"Yes."

He starts to saw himself in and out. I moan at the delicious heat his velvet hardness stokes.

"There's a problem with what I said, though," he says as he comes to a stop, his cock buried as far as it can go at this angle. "You know what it is, Bridge?"

I don't exactly remember what he said. What is he referring to? Not able to come up with an answer, I shake my head.

"This pussy," he says as he withdraws before slamming into me, making me gasp, "isn't yours."

I cry out again when he slams into me a second time.

"It's. Mine."

He shoves his cock deep several times. His pelvis slaps into my rump, jarring me. I love and hate it all at once.

"Oh…shit!" I swear when he plunges in extra hard.

Even though my heels already have me on my toes, I rise up farther to see if improving the angle will decrease the pain. He pistons his cock into me, picking up the pace and the force till it becomes fast and furious. My teeth are going to chatter out of my mouth, and it feels as if he's trying to ram his cock through my pussy and out the top of my head.

"M-Mercy," I say.

He slows and winds a hand through my hair.

"You think you get a safe word?" he asks into my ear. "Only good subs deserve safe words."

He bites my earlobe as my heart sinks. "Bad subs just get fucked."

He kisses, mouths, and bites my neck before resuming his attempts to split me in half. His hand is still fisted in my hair, causing my back to arch. I have nothing to brace myself against, nothing to deaden the blow of being impaled upon his cock in a blinding blur. Even the rope is an accomplice, chafing my wrists as I desperately try to put some daylight between our bodies.

Just when I think I might break down in sobs, he slows. Letting go of my hair, he drops his hand between my thighs and strokes my clit. I whimper with relief. His other hand gropes a breast through my dress. My breasts feel extra heavy and seem to yearn toward his touch. His fingers against my clit are heaven-sent, especially after the brutal pounding. I'm surprised my arousal has survived the battering, but I feel the promise of bliss flit through me like beautiful butterflies tempting the eye.

I feel his cock flex inside of me. The fullness combined with the strumming of his fingers is so delicious, despite the soreness of my poor pussy, my orgasm looms.

But before I can ascend the peak, Darren stops. "You want to taste yourself?"

Without waiting for my response, he cups the side of my face and jams his fingers between my lips. I lick and suck his digits. He grunts. Pulling out his cock, he presses it against that other hole.

My heart stops. If he goes as hard there as he did in my pussy, he's going to rip me a new one. But a part of me is so desperate to come, I almost don't care as long as he'll let me finish.

Please be gentle, I want to say, but his fingers are still in my mouth.

He pushes his tip into me. I will my body to relax. His cock breaches the initial resistance of my sphincter. I gasp, but it's not too bad so far. The hard part, however, is coming.

He sinks deeper. My pussy, feeling empty, throbs in jealousy. My anus, however, would be happy to trade places. Even with my wetness as a lubricant, the stretching feels a little rough. I breath through it as if I'm giving birth.

Just when I think he's gone as far as he can, he pushes a little farther.

"Oh, baby, that feels good," he mutters when he finally seems content with how much of him is now lodged in my butt. "That feel good to you, Bridge? You like your ass stuffed with my cock?"

"Mmhmm," I whimper, still trying to get used to the fullness.

Luckily for me, he keeps a slow pace as he begins to thrust. I grunt and cry, but as long as he doesn't go too hard or fast, I can get used to it. His other hand reaches for my clit, and my ardor does somersaults. Desire churns in my loins.

Please let me come.

I want to beg, but I don't dare. According to him, I don't deserve to come. I don't want to upset him just by asking. Plus, I probably need his permission to come. That's how it worked when we were playing.

Only I don't know if I can hold it back. All those old sensations are returning, and my body wants it. It wants to come undone. His cock is hitting the right spot. His fondling pushes me toward the edge. My efforts to stem the tide of desire have me trembling. I worry I might bite his fingers. Maybe he won't notice me coming if he comes first. He's getting closer, based on the crescendo of his grunts and groans and the fact that he's driving into me harder. I don't mind anymore because the only thing that matters is coming. I mean, not coming. I just need to—

My orgasm bursts through me, shaking me, quaking me. I'm only half aware of Darren drilling into my ass before he, too, is overcome. I feel his liquid heat empty into me.

As the rapture finally settles for the both of us, he gradually disengages from me. I want to drop to my knees, but going limp against the ropes won't feel good. Reality seeps in, and I feel sore and achy in a variety of places.

But Darren came. Which is what I wanted. But now what?

CHAPTER NINETEEN

BRIDGET

Past

"Thank you soooo much for coming to the event with me," Amy gushes, leaning into me as we sit in the back of JD's car. Only this time he and Darren aren't with us.

"I got a little worried the way you were laying in to Eric Drumm," Amy continues, "but it all worked out."

"You guys were gone a while," I say impishly. I'm relieved. I'd feel bad if I had ruined her chances with JD.

"Yeah, well, he wanted to show me his bedroom again."

Even in the dark, I can tell she's blushing.

"So what did you do while I was with JD?" Amy asks. "Harass Eric Drumm some more?"

"I should have," I reply. "But I just hung out with Darren."

"Just the two of you?"

"Yeah," I say.

"Don't tell me you two got it on?"

My mind flashes back to the foot massage he gave me. Holy crap that was...unusual, amazing, distressing.

"No!" I protest and shift in my seat. I glance out the window as the car pulls onto the Bay Bridge on its way back to campus.

"Did you at least try?"

"I doubt I'm his type. And he's not exactly mine."

Could he tell I was about to orgasm? How embarrassing would that be? He'd think I was some kind of freak. Though, why should I care if he did? It sounded like Amy and JD had made enough progress that she wouldn't need me anymore.

"Why not?" Amy challenged. "He's super-hot. He's filthy rich. What else do you need?"

"Personality. Intelligence. A good heart."

"Well, sure. But he and JD both went to UCLA, so they're not stupid."

"Men can have prestigious degrees and still be idiots. Just look at Drumm."

"I don't think he's an idiot. You just don't like his politics."

"Okay, maybe he's not an idiot. He's worse than an idiot: like his dad, he lacks a solid moral compass. He's all bluster and no substance."

Amy sinks into the leather seat. "Ugh."

"Seriously. I fear for this country if Drumm is elected."

"How did we end up talking about Drumm? I thought we were talking about Darren."

Shoot. Drumm was a much more comfortable subject matter for me to dig into. Darren Lee? Not comfortable.

"You agree that's he's hot, right?" Amy presses, sitting up.

I squirm, thinking about the moment in the kitchen when he

had me trapped against the refrigerator. I actually thought he might kiss me. Or maybe that was wishful thinking. "I guess."

"It's a simple yes or no question, with the answer being 'yes.'"

"Okay, okay. It's just that he was so rude to me that first time."

"He made a mistake and he said he was sorry. He wasn't rude again, was he?"

"No. We had a decent conversation."

"He didn't try to ditch you to be with someone else?"

"He didn't."

"So he's a nice guy."

I'm not sure about that. I still detect an edge to him, and there's something about JD I can't quite put my finger on. Maybe it's that I doubt he's relationship material.

"It's too early to tell," I answer.

"What'd you guys talk about?"

"His trip to Bali."

"And?"

I give a nervous chuckle. "What's with the third degree?"

"I just don't know how you can be around him and not be, like, hot and bothered all the time. I mean, don't you want to jump his bones? Forget the personality and being nice. That doesn't matter for sex."

"You sure the driver can't hear us?" I ask, looking toward the front of the car.

Amy shrugs but lowers her voice. "Come on. Admit you find him attractive."

"I thought we already agreed he's really hot."

Amy smiles broadly. "We agreed he's hot. You added the 'really.'"

I give her a playful shove.

"So all you did was talk?"

I hesitate. Part of me wants to share with Amy. But I don't know that I want her encouraging anything with Darren. It's probably best I forget him.

"We cleaned up," I offer.

"Oh. Weren't there people to do that?"

I chew on the nail of my pinky finger. Darren hadn't said anything that would indicate he knew I had come close to climaxing from the foot rub. But that didn't mean he didn't know. What if what he did was intentional? But why would he? I make a mental note to look up foot reflexology when we get home.

Amy narrows her eyes at me. "What's wrong?"

"Nothing."

"You're not telling me something."

I sigh and decide to be forthcoming. "He also gave me a foot massage."

She sits up farther. "That sounds sexy. Or gross. I can't decide when it comes to feet. Was it good?"

"Honestly? It felt amazing. I've never really gotten a massage before. Well, one of my ex-boyfriends rubbed my neck and shoulders, but it was nothing like what Darren did."

She grins at me. "Now I'm curious. I should ask JD for a

massage."

Taking the chance to turn the attention away from myself, I ask, "So how far did you two go, if you don't mind my asking? 'Course if you don't want to kiss and tell—"

"Pbbff. Why wouldn't I? It's so much fun to kiss and tell! I mean, it was just a quickie because, you know, he had guests downstairs, but we went all the way."

Her eyes are shining.

I inquire, "So I take it you want to see him again?"

"Of course!"

"Did he say anything about getting together again?"

"He said he'll call or text me."

Famous last words from a lot of men. But I keep my mouth shut. Amy prattles on about JD, musing where they might go on an official date and what she might wear.

When we get back to our place, I hop on my computer and look up reflexology.

So sexual reflexology *is* a thing, and a foot rub isn't the only way to influence the sex organs. I spend way too much time reading up about acupressure and traditional Chinese medicine, the basis for the practice of reflexology. By the time I make it to bed, I'm hot and bothered. I want the orgasm I missed out on earlier, and when I hear Amy has fallen asleep, I sneak my hand beneath the covers.

The climax from masturbating doesn't feel as intense as the one I could have had, and I'm only partially satisfied.

Damn Darren Lee.

CHAPTER TWENTY

DARREN

Past

"You didn't want to drive them back yourself?" I ask JD after he had sent Amy and Bridget off with his driver in the Cullinan.

"Nah," JD replies as he flops down on the sofa Bridget and I occupied earlier. "Already scored with her tonight. Plus, I didn't want to waste your time dragging you over to Berkeley."

"You don't give a shit about wasting my time," I say as I sit down opposite him. "So, you gonna see her again?"

JD opens his cigarette case and lights one. "You mean Amy?"

"No, I was referring to Oprah Winfrey."

After blowing out a long trail of smoke, he replies, "Yeah, I think so. I mean, she's pretty damn cute. And I didn't get to see her completely naked. Sorry you got stuck with her roommate for so long. I didn't think she'd bring the same friend again."

I don't believe JD is that sorry, but I say, "It wasn't so bad."

"You're a trooper, bro. I promise it'll just be me and Amy next time."

I consider the prospect of never seeing Bridget again. It's probably for the best. I don't need to spend time with some bleeding heart who will make me feel guilty if I don't spend every spare penny helping someone in need.

Would have been cool to see her climax, though.

"It's actually kind of fun messing with her," I say.

JD rolls his eyes. "I thought she would never shut up about that hunting endangered species shit."

I lean back into the sofa and put my hands behind my head, smiling as I recall Eric frowning in discomfort. "Maybe Eric had it coming to him."

"You're not on her side, are you?"

"I don't know what it is about the guy that rubs me the wrong way."

"You're a businessman. You've got to look past that shit. It's worth putting up with him because it'll pay dividends later."

"What if his dad doesn't win the election? He hasn't even made it past the primary."

JD draws on his cigarette before answering, "It's a low-risk gamble. What's the worst-case scenario? I lose a couple grand supporting his dad's election bid."

"He wants us to invest in his resort."

"Yeah, but it'll help us stand out from the rest of his donors." He puts out the cigarette. "Want to head over to the club? I told Olga I might swing by."

"You're going to get with Olga the same night you did it with Amy?"

JD gives me a what-are-you-talking-about look. "Why the hell not?"

*****

The following morning, the woman next to me in bed stirs against me and the first thing that flashes through my head is Bridget.

Fucking Bridget Moore.

The play session I had last night at The Lotus wasn't bad, and I thought it would be good enough to kick Bridget out of my system. She's the one who didn't come during the foot massage, so why am I the one who feels incomplete?

"You want breakfast?" I ask Emma.

She snuggles closer to me, puts her hand beneath the covers and squeezes my cock. "You bet I do."

I roll her beneath me and within minutes, I'm thrusting away inside her. Usually I take more time between getting to the meat of the action, but I need to get Bridget out of my head.

Only it doesn't work. I manage to hold off until Emma comes, but throughout it all, I kept wondering what it would be like to have Bridget writhing beneath me.

After I've dressed and seen Emma off, I head back inside The Lotus and check in with Cheryl. We sit at the bar as she goes over access requests, staffing updates, a new supplier who wants our business, and that Manny Wu had called her when he couldn't get through to me.

"I helped him out the other day," I say. "What does he want now?"

"He's asking if he can bring a guy named Tim Tran tonight," Cheryl replies.

"Who's that?"

"I looked into him. He runs with the Park Street Boyz in the Tenderloin."

I frown. The PSB have had run-ins with the *Jing San* in the past. "Why is Manny interested in this guy?"

"He didn't say. Wants to talk to you about it."

"All right. I'll call him back. Anything else?"

Cheryl hands me a shopping bag, the kind one gets from a boutique.

"What's this?" I ask, not expecting a present.

"A sweater. Came back from the dry cleaner's."

I look in the bag. The beige garment is immediately familiar to me.

"Should we just toss it?" Cheryl asks.

I think for a moment, then take the bag. "I'll get it back to its owner."

After Cheryl goes into her office, I call Manny. "You're joking, right? The Park Street Boyz?"

"I know, I know," Manny says. "But that's in the past."

"Not everyone thinks so."

"But even the old-timers understand a good opportunity when they see one."

"Yeah?"

"You know Tran runs a few massage parlors here, South San Francisco and Daly City, right? Well, we can move even farther down the Peninsula, expand into the suburbs."

I grab the bag with the sweater and continue the conversation as I make way down to the garage. "What does that have to do with my club?"

"I thought I'd make a good impression with Tran."

"Take him to a nice restaurant."

"I want somewhere we can talk business, too. Besides, your club is better than any restaurant."

"There's too much history with the PSB."

"Those old turf wars are a thing of the past. It's more about racism than anything else. Just 'cause the PSB are mostly Southeast Asians, the old stiffs think they're low-level shit."

"The PSB are a street gang with no finesse. They pick fights in the open and that draws the attention of law enforcement."

"Come on, Darren," Manny whines. "This is a good opportunity for me."

I think for a moment before relenting. "One time."

"Darren, you're the best!"

Hanging up, I open the door to my Porsche and place the bag with the sweater inside. I should have Cheryl figure out a way to get it to Bridget by courier or next-day delivery. But it's an excuse to see Bridget again.

But first I have a meeting with Eric Drumm for lunch so he can pitch me on his resort project. JD and I meet with him at a restaurant that serves Asian haute cuisine.

"This is crazy shit," Eric says as he looks over the menu. "Can you charge these kinds of prices for what's basically an egg roll and fried rice? I mean, what's next? Hundred-dollar tacos?"

"You suggesting ethnic food can't be fancy?" I ask instead of pointing out that he chose the restaurant to begin with.

"I'm saying food shouldn't pretend to be something it's not. I wouldn't pay fifty dollars for a Big Mac, no matter how fancy you make it."

"I would," JD says. "Just out of curiosity."

Eric chuckles. "Yeah, you're right."

He looks down at the silver chopsticks tied with a ribbon and set on the napkin. "This place has forks, doesn't it? Never understood chopsticks. I get that it's cultural, but why stick with it when there's a superior utensil?"

"Because the fork isn't superior," I say.

Eric scrunches up his face in a what-the-hell-you-talking-about way.

"Can you pick up a single grain of rice with a fork?" I ask.

"Who would want to pick up a single grain of rice? It would take you fucking forever to finish a meal that way."

I can understand Bridget's desire to call this guy out. There's something obnoxious about him, though it's subtle, so I can't put my finger on exactly why I don't like him.

Through the course of lunch, JD and I listen to Eric brag about how spectacular his golf and spa resort in Northern California is going to be and the many successes he and his

149

father have had developing resorts.

"But I don't have to give you all the details," Eric says as he jabs his fork into a potsticker. "The Drumm name is a known commodity. Nobody does resorts like us. This is a once-in-a-lifetime opportunity to get in on the ground floor."

I'm glad when lunch finally comes to a close.

"Hey, I've got to run to my next meeting," Eric says, "but let's talk again. And thanks again for the fundraiser last night."

Shortly after he leaves, the server arrives to leave the tab.

I turn to JD. "The fucker invites us out to lunch and leaves us with the bill?"

Without looking at the tab, JD tosses his credit card onto the little silver platter it came with. "What, you can't afford lunch all of a sudden?"

"I don't give a shit about a few hundred dollars, but it's not like Drumm is hurting for money. Guess I'm old fashioned. He wants to make it to third base with me on this resort proposal, he should at least put out for lunch."

"You *are* old fashioned, bro. So you in on this golf and spa thing?"

"Tony already met with him and turned him down," I remind him.

JD looks up at the ceiling at the mention of Tony's name. "He's supposedly all legit now. Didn't have what it takes to stay."

"Might be worth talking to him to hear his take."

"You gonna call Benjamin Lee next?"

"He *is* a developer. We're not. What do we know about resorts? Hell, I don't even play golf."

Hearing his phone ding, JD takes it out and checks the text that came in. He smiles. "Aww, how cute."

He shows me a Bitmoji Amy has sent him, saying she hopes he's having a great day.

"When are you seeing her again?" I ask.

"Haven't decided. Olga asked if I was free. You don't mind, do you? I mean, if you do, you can have first dibs. Or we can share her."

"Go for it. I don't mind."

"You sure?"

I think I'll return the sweater myself. It would make sense for me to get Bridget's number before driving over to Berkeley, but I've got nothing scheduled for the afternoon.

"I'm sure," I reply.

CHAPTER TWENTY-ONE

BRIDGET

Past

After lacing up my running shoes, I grab the grocery list. Normally I'd borrow Amy's car to go grocery shopping, but she took it to work, and I've decided the nice autumn weather would make for a good jog down to Trader Joe's.

"Can you grab me some of those mini ice cream cones?" Simone asks from the living room sofa as I head out.

"They might melt on the way back," I reply. "I don't have Amy's car today."

"Bummer. I love those mini ice cream cones. I go through a box of them in like two days."

I like those cones, too, but the walk back from the store will take over an hour.

As I head down the stairs, I pass by Kiera. With her iPhone strapped to her arm, she must have come back from jogging. Her sneakers are immaculately white, and she wears brightly colored, form-fitting leggings and a strappy top. Even I can tell the clothes are high end as far as workout clothes go, in sharp contrast to the bike shorts and baggy sweatshirt I'm wearing.

Kiera sees me but doesn't say anything.

Before I hit the sidewalk, I make sure my phone, debit card and keys are securely zipped in the pocket of my sweatshirt, then realize I don't have my grocery list with me. I check my pockets again, then look around me to see if it fell out. Although the list is fairly short, I want it because I don't want to forget to get pepper.

"Hey."

Looking up, I see that it's Darren Lee, leaning against his silver car. I wonder that I didn't notice it before because it's probably the fanciest vehicle on the entire street. And Darren, wearing a button-up shirt and black slacks, is the hottest-looking thing on the street.

"Hi," I reply, half expecting to see JD with him. "Amy's at work."

"I came over to give you back your sweater," he explains before reaching into his car and pulling out a bag.

"Oh, thanks," I say in surprise as I take the bag and look inside to see that the sweater is neatly folded and even tied with a ribbon.

"It's been cleaned," he tells me.

"You didn't have to—how much do I owe you?" I ask, hoping the cleaning bill isn't too high.

"Nothing."

I should insist on paying him back. "Really. It's—"

"It's no big deal." He looks me over. "Where you headed?"

"The grocery store."

"I'll give you a lift."

I blink several times. Why is he being nice to me?

"You don't—" I begin.

Clearly not expecting a refusal, he opens the passenger door. The Trader Joe's is on his way if he's headed back to the city, but he doesn't know that's where I intend to shop.

"Get in," he tells me.

To my own chagrin, I do as he says. It's the path of least resistance, though I don't want him thinking that I'll always obey his commands.

"What's the store?" he asks after he gets in the driver's seat.

"Trader Joe's. It's on University."

He repeats the info to his car. A map shows up on the windshield.

"Whoa," I gasp.

Still feeling leftover awkwardness from the foot massage, I search for something to say. "Nice car."

As he pulls the car away from the curb, I roll my eyes at myself. I could have come up with something better than that. Plus, I don't want him thinking I care what kind of car he drives.

"It's a Panamera," he says.

Since that means nothing to me, I reply, "Oh."

He gives me a sidelong glance. "You don't know what a Panamera is, do you?"

"I don't know anything about cars, really. This one seems nice.

And expensive."

"It was just a hundred K. But you're not impressed."

"Why? Should I be? It's a just car."

"Just a car?" he repeats with skepticism.

"I mean, I get that cars mean more to a guy than a means of transportation. It's a penis extender, right?"

He stares at me. "For some guys, sure."

"But not for you?" I brave.

Turning his gaze back toward the road, he seems to chuckle to himself. "You wouldn't believe me no matter what I say."

There's only way to find out.

I quickly pull my mind out of the gutter and try to think of something else to talk about.

"Some guys care about cars because women care about cars," he adds.

"No, we don't. You know what my dream car is? A Honda Accord, because it's a good value, fuel efficient and lasts a long time. Though if I can afford it, I'd get an electric version."

His car tells him to turn down University Avenue.

"Let's say you can afford any car you wanted—" Darren starts.

"I'd still get a Honda Accord."

"Why?"

"Because I don't need anything fancier. I'd rather spend whatever extra money I had on something else."

155

"Like feeding the homeless?"

"Yeah."

"You think that now because you don't know what it's like to have a lot of disposable income."

"I can't imagine what I would do with a fancy car that I couldn't do with a Honda Accord except show it off. But the sort of people who would care what kind of car I drive are not the sort of shallow people I want to know."

"That's harsh. Are you saying people shouldn't treat themselves to something like a nice car? They have to end world hunger first?"

I knit my brows in thought, but eventually respond, "Why not? The world would be better off if a few less fancy cars meant more kids didn't have to go hungry."

He turns silent.

"I'm sorry," I say. "Are you feeling guilty about your Porsche?"

He looks over at me. "I wasn't until I met you."

"I'm sorry. I think."

"You said you wished you could do something special for your grandmother, like treat her to a dinner cruise. Those cost, what, a hundred or two? Shouldn't you be giving that money to those more in need?"

I see his point. A dinner cruise is a luxury for many in the world.

"Does it have to be all or nothing?" he asks. "Or can you treat yourself once in a while and still be a do-gooder?"

I peer at him. "Are you a do-gooder sometimes?"

He frowns and stares ahead. "No."

"At least you're honest."

He doesn't say anything. I try to lift the suddenly solemn mood. "You returned my sweater to me. That was a nice deed."

"That's patronizing."

"Some people have to start small," I object. "You're the one who said you don't do any good."

"Yeah, well, there's also nothing intrinsically virtuous about being poor or depriving yourself."

I nod and decide to change the subject. "So you were in the area?" I couldn't resist asking. I know it's probably far-fetched to think he'd make a special trip just for me, but I want confirmation.

He looks at me. "What do you mean, was I 'in the area?'"

He's got to know what I mean. Is he trying to get me to say it out loud?

"Like, what were you doing in Berkeley?" I rephrase.

"Returning your sweater."

His stare makes me squirm. I change the subject again. "So what do you like about this car? I'm guessing it's not the fuel efficiency."

"It extends my penis by three inches."

I look at him in surprise, then laugh. "Only three? For a hundred thousand, I would expect at least a five-inch gain. You got gypped."

He chuckles. "Good thing it has other qualities I care about. It drives smooth. I like the way it looks. Fuel efficiency isn't bad since it's a hybrid."

I smile. "Hey, there's hope for you yet."

He pulls into the parking garage of the Trader Joe's and we get out. I remember I still haven't found my list, so I'll have to go off memory. Once inside the store, I grab a shopping cart and head to the produce aisle for collard greens and sweet potato.

"You cook?" he asks as he follows me about the store.

"A little. Aunt Coretta was a fantastic cook, and she would let me help her."

"This was your neighbor and grandmother's friend?"

"Yeah, she helped raise me. I'm making her collard greens recipe tonight. Do you cook?"

"No."

"At all?"

"Why, if I don't have to?"

I shake my head and put a ham hock into the cart. "You're such a millennial."

"You're a millennial, too."

"Cooking is fun."

"Cooking is work."

"That, too," I admitted. "But it's a basic skill everyone should know to some degree. You at least know how to boil an egg, right?"

He stares at me without a word.

I realize he doesn't know how to boil an egg. This boy needs help. "Okay, as a favor since you returned my sweater, I'll teach you how to boil an egg."

"After we're done shopping."

I was joking, but he's taking my offer seriously. Too surprised to think coherently, I say, "Well, um, I was going to work on my resume tonight. There's this fellowship I want to apply for. Plus, I have to type up some notes on a meeting for my internship."

"How long does it take to boil an egg?"

"Depends on the method and egg size. For hard-boiled eggs, usually about ten minutes."

"I'm a quick learner. You only have to show me once."

He wants to take an egg-boiling lesson from me. Maybe he wasn't just in the area? My pulse has quickened. He's also standing really close to me, rattling my breath.

"Um, okay," I say. It would seem selfish of me not to spare ten minutes of my time when he drove over to give me my sweater and took me grocery shopping.

He reaches for me, and my heart leaps like it's doing the high jump in the Olympics.

But no, he's just reaching for something on the shelf behind me.

"I'm out of salt," he says.

I tell myself to get it together and continue the shopping. We pass by the frozen aisle, and now that I'm getting a ride back to the apartment, I can get Simone's ice cream cones.

"So what are you cooking besides the collard greens?" he asks me as I place the groceries on the counter before the cashier.

"Sweet potato pie with fresh whipped cream."

He looks impressed.

"It's actually really easy—no, I've got this." Seeing him take out his wallet, I slide in front of him and jam my debit card into the machine.

"But my salt—"

"It's just one item."

We check out and head back to the car. I admire the way he navigates the car through the tight quarters of the garage with other cars waiting to grab our parking spot when we pull out.

"So who did the cooking when you were growing up?" I ask as he drives up University Avenue.

"The family chef."

"Did your mom cook?"

"She wasn't a fan of cooking."

"I guess it must be nice to have your meals prepared for you, but you're still missing out."

He lifts a doubtful eyebrow, then says, "I have other interests."

"Like what?"

"The club."

"And?"

"Watching my alma mater crush Cal in football."

"You wish."

"The only thing better is beating Stanford or 'SC."

"We're agreed on that. But football is only once a week. What do you like to do for fun the rest of the time? What's your favorite thing to do?"

He doesn't say anything.

"You've got to have a favorite activity," I urge.

"Sure, but you don't want to know what it is."

"Well, if you put it that way, I totally want to know. Unless it's beating up defenseless puppies. I'd have to report you to the authorities for that."

He stares at me, making me shift in my seat.

"Seriously, what is it?" I prod.

He turns his gaze back to the road. "Like I said, you don't want to know."

Damn. What could it possibly be?

"So, it's either gross, illegal, or embarrassing," I muse aloud.

"Or maybe I just don't want another guilt trip."

Fair enough. I drop the subject.

"What's your internship with?"

I perk up. "It's this coalition that's trying to end poverty in the county."

"Do-gooder stuff."

"Yes! And they're doing such cool initiatives. They're involved in urban farming, food as medicine—"

"What's that?"

I explain to him how a lot of chronic illness in this country can be attribute to lifestyle choices, how low-income families don't have easy access to basic things like fresh produce, and how processed foods can contain ingredients that disrupt gut health. By the time we pull up to my apartment, I'm only partway through my spiel.

I take a break to comment on his good parking karma. Usually it's not so easy finding parking in this part of Berkeley. As we get out of the car, two guys I know from my stats class walk by.

"Sweet ride," one of them says.

"That the kind of accolade you like getting with your Porsche?" I ask as Darren pulls the grocery bags from the trunk.

"I bought the Panamera because *I* like the car," Darren replies, walking over to where I stand next to the car. "I don't give a shit what other people think of it. And, contrary to what you might believe, I don't need a fancy car to compensate for anything."

"Oh, really?" I tease.

Grocery bags in one hand, he braces his free arm against the car, enclosing me. It's just like the moment in Trader Joe's, only there's no salt behind me.

His voice is low and husky, making my pulse skitter. "Really."

I suddenly remember I forgot the pepper.

CHAPTER TWENTY-TWO

DARREN

Past

I don't know what's wrong with me. Maybe it's because I want to pound this judgey disapproval she has of me out of her. All of a sudden I want to drop the groceries and maul her against my car. I want to feel her squirming beneath me. I want to taste her lips. She might let me, too. Her breath is uneven. The pupils in her eyes have dilated. Yeah, she wants to be kissed.

But I say when. I say where. I say how.

Suppressing my desire, I back off. She collects herself, trying to pretend nothing happened, that she didn't get all flustered by my proximity. We walk a block to her apartment building and head up the stairs.

"It's not the Ritz Carlton, but it's rent-controlled," she explains as she unlocks the door.

I doubt anything in this neighborhood comes close to being the Ritz Carlton, but there are some nice, albeit old, homes a few blocks away that are valued at more than a million or two.

"I room with Amy and two other girls," Bridget says.

We walk into what I consider a small space. There's a mural

of what might be African goddesses on the main living room wall.

"Simone's an artist," Bridget explains.

"Your landlord approves of improvements like this?" I ask.

"We'll paint over it if we have to."

I follow her into a kitchen that's barely large enough to fit the two of us.

"You want your egg-boiling lesson now?" she inquires as she unpacks the bags.

"Sure," I answer, half wondering what I'm doing here.

She bends over to put the collard greens in the bottom bin of the refrigerator, inadvertently giving me a view of her ass. It's got a nice curve to it. Definitely spank-worthy.

After putting away the groceries, she grabs a carton of eggs. "Put the eggs in the pot first, then cover it with water."

She demonstrates, covers the pot with a lid, and puts it on the stove.

"How long before it boils?"

"Depends on the stove and the cookware. You want something to drink? We've got zero-calorie cola, sparkling water, and iced tea."

"Where are your roommates?"

"Kat spends most of her time at her boyfriend's place. Amy's at work, and Simone might be in her bedroom."

My cellphone rings. It's Tony Lee.

"I should get this," I say as I walk out to the living room.

I watch Bridget pour herself an iced tea while Tony says, "So you met with Eric Drumm."

"Yeah," I answer. "I called 'cause he said he met with you a few months back."

"C'est vraiment un trou de cul, celui-là."

I don't speak French, but I catch the key word in his statement and reply ironically, "So you like him."

"The resort is a vanity project. It's shit. You won't see a dime. Even Virginia questioned it."

"Who's Virginia?"

"Girl I met. She's just a college student, but she figured him out. Anyway, I asked for Ben's input on the project. He said the Drumm family is all smoke and mirrors. They're in a lot of debt, and he thinks they'll siphon money from this project to pump into their other failing resorts."

"JD and I aren't looking for ROI from the resort itself."

"Your call, but I don't trust the *connard*."

There's an edge to his tone that suggests his distaste for Eric is personal.

Not seeing Bridget anywhere, I wander down the hall to look for her. I find her in her bedroom, bent over her desk, trying to reach for something behind it.

Fuck me.

A picture of me standing behind her, doing her in that position, flashes through my mind. Shaking it away, I tell Tony to hold and ask her, "Need some help?"

"I got it," she mumbles. A second later, she stand back up and lets out a breath. "The outlet is right behind the desk, unfortunately. I'd put the desk elsewhere, but as you can see, there's not a lot of options."

She's right. Between the two beds, two desks, and a dresser, very little room is left.

"You can use this room for your call if you want some privacy," she offers.

I shake my head and turn my attention back to Tony. "So you're passing on an opportunity to get in good with the Drumm family?"

"Not worth it."

"Your brother think the same way?"

"No, he's pissed as hell with me. I was supposed to make friends with Eric, but I'd rather eat shit."

That's a stronger statement than I'd expected. Something happened between the two of them, but I don't want to get into it right now.

"Thanks for the feedback," I say and end the call.

"More fundraising for Drumm?" Bridget asks.

"He wants me to invest in a resort he plans to build upstate."

"Don't do it."

Taken aback by her bluntness, I protest, "You don't know anything about the project."

"Don't have to. Don't you read the news about him and his family? How they always find some excuse not to pay their contractors the full amount? And they never use the larger construction firms. They use little guys whom they can bully around. And they're hypocrites. The senior Drumm makes such a big deal about limiting immigration, but his resorts employ undocumented workers who are too frightened to advocate for themselves."

"Governor Drumm could be the next president."

"So you're going to overlook his faults because of that?"

"In business—hell, in life—you have to overlook a lot of things."

She shakes her head. "There's got to be better people to do business with. Let's say Drumm does become president. What are you hoping to get out of it?"

"Nothing. For myself. But I have family and friends who are interested."

I keep to myself the fact that the president appoints the Attorney General, the FBI Director, etcetera. The *Jing San* has lower-level connections in these government agencies, but we're looking to aim higher.

"That's nice of you to be supporting your family and friends," Bridget says, "and I'd hope they'd understand if you wanted to make a business decision based on principles other than political gain."

I lean against the doorframe and cross my arms. "What makes you think I have any principles?"

She furrows her brow. I want to point out that she can't name anything.

"Just a gut feeling, I guess," she finally says, looking straight into my eyes.

I don't like it, this 'gut feeling' of hers. Maybe because you can't reason with feelings. Maybe something else. Straightening, I advance toward her. "What if I told you I don't have any kind of principles? Not the sort that you would like anyway. That I don't have a do-gooder bone in my body?"

Surprised by my response, she unconsciously backs away, but in this small bedroom, there's nowhere to go. The back of her legs bump against her twin-sized bed.

"You had my sweater cleaned," she says. "That was a good deed."

I stand right in front of her. "I didn't do anything. You can thank Cheryl, my manager."

"Well, you apologized for being rude about my sweater."

"Did I?"

"And you let us have drinks on the house—that was nice."

"Maybe I just wanted to help JD score points with Amy."

She looks down, searching for a response. I cup her chin and lift her gaze to mine. How did I not notice before that her eyes were so pretty? Guess 'cause I'm usually looking at other parts of the body.

"You didn't have to return my sweater," she says hastily, as if that will get me to back away. "You didn't have to give me a lift to the grocery store. That was nice of you."

If she knew what was going through my mind, the sorts of things I'd like to do to her, she would not think me nice.

"Is it 'nice' if I had ulterior motives?" I return, sliding my thumb along her lower lip.

Her breath quivers, making the blood throb in the area of my groin.

"Ul—Ulterior motives?"

"It probably wasn't such a good idea to invite me up to your place," I say, talking to both myself and her.

"What kind of ulterior motives?"

I could go there. Would she stop me? Maybe, maybe not. But for my own sake, I back off. A little. "Like finishing the foot massage."

"We weren't done?"

You weren't done. But aloud I say, releasing her, "No, we weren't."

"Oh, well um, Simone's in her room. She's got her door closed, but…"

"But? What are you worried about?"

"Nothing."

I sit down on the bed. "Okay, then."

She thinks for a moment, decides to close the door, then sits on the bed beside me. I pull up her legs and lay them across my lap. I unlace her shoes and pull them off, followed by her socks.

"Giving someone a foot massage is a nice thing to do," she says as I start to rub one foot.

Ulterior motive, I remind her silently. But I hang back. I don't have to go further than a foot massage. I *should* just go back to The Lotus and hang out with a woman who only asks superficial questions and won't criticize my lack of woke-ness.

Bridget is tense and nervous. I can feel it in her body. But she could have passed on the foot massage, so the fact that she didn't means she wants this.

"Maybe that's the only nice thing I'm capable of," I say as I dig my thumb into her stiffness.

"You can't be all that bad. You obviously care a lot about your cousin."

"If you're trying to find redeeming qualities in me, your search isn't going to go very far."

"Why are you trying to convince me that you're bad?"

To warn you. Nice girls like you get burned by guys like me.

"Oh, I get it," she continues. "You like to project a 'bad boy' image."

"I sure as hell can't project a 'good boy' image if I'm not that. Turn around."

"What?"

"Lay on your stomach and relax."

She hesitates but does as I say, laying her head on her pillow. "So how did you get into foot reflexology?"

"I had it done to me in Bali. And my girlfriend at the time really liked it."

"Was that girlfriend Kimberly?"

"Yes."

"I did some web research on reflexology."

"Yeah?"

"It's…interesting."

I look over the length of her body, wondering what it would feel like beneath mine.

She starts asking mundane questions: do I see a regular reflexologist, what else did I like about Bali, do I try other forms of TCM? I keep my answers short and eventually she stops talking as she sinks into the massage.

Once she's completely relaxed, I start to home in on the sexual points. She muffles a giggle.

"We're finishing this time," I tell her.

She nods, then buries her face into the pillow. I sense the shift in her body, the blossom of energy. Her body shudders. The pillow muffles what might be a groan, gasp or laugh. I move to a different part of her foot. She remains prone and quiet. After a few more minutes, I set down her feet. I need to adjust the crotch of my pants but don't move so as not to disturb her.

"That was…" she murmurs.

Slowly she sits up. Her cheeks are slightly flushed, her eyes are bright. She tucks her hair behind her ear. "Thanks." She swings her legs over the side of the bed. "You're, um, really good. Like, you could be a professional masseuse."

So she's not going to acknowledge the orgasm she had. It doesn't bother me, though. She knows it happened. I know it happened.

"Should we check on the eggs?" I ask.

She leaps up and scrambles out the room. I follow her into the kitchen.

"I almost burnt the pot," she says, showing me there is just a little bit of water left.

"The Lotus opens in less than two hours, and I've got to greet someone there," I tell her. "We can redo the cooking lesson later. I can have JD's driver pick up you and Amy."

"Later *tonight*?"

"Just text me when Amy's done at work. Around ten o'clock."

She bristles, probably taken aback by the fact that I didn't *ask* her to come over and instead *told* her she would. 'Course, she could simply object.

"I'll have to see," she replies. "I was going to work on my resume and type up those notes."

Not allowing her that out, I say, "You have time between now and ten."

She sucks in her breath.

I stare down at her. "If you're good, you can earn another foot massage."

As I expected, she doesn't know how to respond to that.

I take my leave and close the door behind me. I let out a large breath. Coming over probably wasn't the best idea. Now the only way to get her out of my system is to fuck the crap out of her.

CHAPTER TWENTY-THREE

BRIDGET

Past

Darren's left, but I'm still in a daze. I can't believe I orgasmed from a foot rub. Does he know I orgasmed? Was that foot rub considered sex, since I climaxed?

I salvage the boiled eggs and put them in ice water. What in the world am I doing? I've never moved this fast with a guy before. And I'm pretty sure I didn't even like him to begin with. Hell, do I like him now? He's not my type. Not by a long shot. And I don't like the way he just assumed I'd want to go over to his club tonight. He's probably used to women tripping over him, so he expects I will, too.

Only he's the one who sought *me* out. And why is that? Was he, for real, interested in me? And what's my interest in him aside from the fact that my body has a way of responding to his presence and his touch?

Deciding that I'm overthinking things, I go into my room and try to focus on my resume. It's not easy at first, but I turn on some music and eventually find my stride. In fact, I've got a draft done by the time Amy calls me.

"Hey, JD says he's sending his driver to come pick us up,"

Amy tells me. "I worked it out so that I can leave my shift early. It's going to take me a while to figure out what to wear."

"Which reminds me that I don't have any club-appropriate clothing."

"Borrow something from Simone again."

"She's taller than me. I have to wear heels to compensate."

"So borrow a skirt or dress."

I sigh. I like wearing my own clothes. And I'm not a fan of skirts or dresses, but I go ahead and ask Simone what she has.

"I'm not really a skirt or dress person, either," Simone tells me. "I have a jean skirt and this black thing, which I think works well for clubbing."

The dress, a black halter with a low neckline, is a little fancy to pair with my Mary Jane flats, but I take it.

"What kind of bra do you wear with it?" I ask.

"You don't. You want some earrings to go with the dress?"

Simone likes large earrings with a lot of dazzle. Since I'm not looking to stand out in the crowd, I shake my head. "Thanks for the dress, though. Hopefully this is the last time I'll have to borrow clothes from you."

"Don't sweat it. This guy must be special. I've never seen you dress up for anyone before."

My heart skips a beat. "I'm just providing Amy company."

Simone raises her beautifully arched brows. "So you don't have a thing with that hunk of yum who was here earlier?"

"What?"

"I heard our front door close, then saw him walk away from our building from my window."

"How could you tell what he looked like?"

"He turned around after he caught ahold of Jordan. He was walking one way, and she the other. She conveniently tripped right when they passed each other. And she was flirting like you wouldn't believe." Simone rolled her eyes. She wasn't a fan of Jordan either.

"I guess they'd make a cute couple," I muse aloud.

"What are you talking about? You're not giving up on the guy so easily?" Simone exclaimed. "I mean, he was here, in our apartment, with *you*, for a reason."

"Yeah, it's weird. But guys like Darren only slum it for one reason. Cinderella stories don't exist in real life. Not unless you're a model."

"So if he was just looking for some booty, you wouldn't be interested?"

I wish I could say no, that I wouldn't be interested, but somehow my practical side is on vacation all of a sudden.

"Well, if you decide you're up for just the fun parts, he's a good choice," Simone says with a sly smile.

After hanging up Simone's dress on the back of my door, I decide I have time to go for a short jog and shower. Amy returns while I'm blow-drying my hair.

"It was not easy getting my coworkers to cover for me," Amy tells me as she goes through several different outfits. "Luckily, it's not that busy a night, and it's not like they're going to get a rush of people after eight PM."

From our bedroom window, I can see JD's driver has pulled up in front and double parked. But fifteen minutes go by, and Amy still hasn't settled on what she's going to wear. I go down and inform the driver. It's another chilly night, so I decide to go back up and grab my thick sweater.

"You're not seriously wearing that thing?" Amy asks. "After I threw up on it? I would have burned the thing."

"It keeps me warm," I reply. "And it seems clean and fresh."

After another fifteen minutes, Amy decides on platform heels and a slinky red cocktail dress.

"Isn't this fun?" she asks when we're finally seated in the car and on our way. "So much better than going to frat parties. Now that I've gotten to know JD, college boys seem like, well, boys."

I haven't been to a frat party in a while, but The Lotus is several steps up, to say the least.

"Can you believe we've been invited to hang out with JD and Darren *three* times this week?" Amy continues while checking her makeup in her compact.

"It's crazy. I never go out this much," I say.

"Yeah, you're not the partying type. So it must be you've got a thing for Darren."

I balk. "I only went to the club and that reception—which I probably wouldn't have gone to if I had known it was a fundraiser for Drumm—to keep you company."

"Okay, but what about tonight? I'm comfortable enough going alone now, especially since I get my own private driver. How awesome is that?"

Once we arrive at The Lotus, JD finds Amy immediately. He slides his arm around her waist. Amy looks like she's in seventh heaven.

"Damn, you look good, girl," he says before turning to me. "Darren'll be down soon. He's on a call with his mother."

"I'll be at the bar," I say.

JD turns back to Amy. "Wanna dance?"

Amy practically skips to the dance floor with JD. I sit down at the bar.

"Hey, you," greets the bartender from my first night here.

"Hi," I say, happy to see a friendly face. "I don't think I ever caught your name. Mine's Bridget."

"Felipe."

We shake hands. He looks at my sweater. "That the same one—?"

"Yeah. Kimberly's not here, is she? If so, you might want to give her a warning. I don't want to be the reason she goes blind. Not completely, anyway."

I grin sheepishly, not having intended those last words to come out.

But Felipe leans in closer. "I know, right? Kimberly is a piece of work. I don't know what Darren saw in her. It's not like he can't get a girl with real boobs that size."

"So he's a tit man?" I ask, thinking about my own breasts, which just manage to fill a B-cup.

Felipe shrugs. "Actually, I've seen him with all kinds of women."

"Well, boobs aren't Kimberly's only assets. She looks like she could be a model."

"Oh, she is one. But even if I were a straight guy, which thankfully I'm not, I still wouldn't go for her. What can I get you? Glass of Coke? Shirley temple?"

"Shirley temple sounds good. I'm impressed you know my drinks."

"You were kind of unforgettable. Even without the Coke-in-the-face incidence."

I feel my cheeks warm. "Oh, *that* little incident. Trust me, I don't do that all the time."

Felipe laughs as he prepares my drink. "I like your spunk. Darren deserved it."

"I'm just glad we worked it out."

I happen to glance down the end of the bar, where a man and a woman are sitting. The man stares at Felipe before turning his attention back to the woman.

"You know much about JD?" I ask as Felipe hands me my drink.

Felipe steals a glance at the man when he's not looking. "What's that?"

"You know JD well?"

"I guess. Enough to know he likes 'em young and petite, like your friend."

"He seems like he could be a player."

Felipe drops his gaze and wipes the counter. "What makes you say that?"

"I don't know. Just a vibe."

"Or women's intuition?"

"Maybe. I just don't want to see my friend hurt."

I see the man at the end of the bar look at Felipe again. Leaning in toward Felipe, I whisper, "I think that guy at the end is checking you out."

It's dark, but it looks like Felipe is blushing. "Really? He's super-hot, but I probably just remind him of someone."

The woman laughs at something the man has said.

"And he looks like he's on a date with that woman," Felipe adds.

"My gay-dar is weak, but there's something about the *way* that he looks at you that makes me think he might be interested," I insist.

The man leaves the bar and heads to the restroom. The woman goes through something in her purse, then decides to head in the same direction.

"Want me to see if I can find out if they're on a date?" I ask.

"No! Well…"

"Be back."

Hopping off the barstool, I follow the woman into the ladies' room. Looking around, I see a woman take an exit on the other side of the bathroom from where I came in. Maybe it leads to an employee area. Spotting the woman from the bar standing in front of a mirror reapplying her lipstick, I go over and pretend to wash my hands at the sink next to her.

"You mind my asking if the guy you're with is single?" I blurt.

Worst case, she's on a date with him and hates me.

She looks me up and down. "I'm afraid he's not your type, sweetie."

"I'm asking for a friend."

"Sure you are. I wouldn't bother if I were you. Bryan doesn't date women."

"So you're not on a date with him?" I ask politely.

"No, I'm not."

"He seemed really interested in you."

"He's after my portfolio. Bryan's an investment banker." She narrows her eyes. "If you thought we were on a date, you've got some nerve asking about him."

I grab one of the fluffy hand towels from the basket. "Like I said, it's for a friend."

Cheerfully, I hurry back to the bar.

Felipe comes over immediately. "So?"

Beaming, I tell him what I learned from the woman.

Felipe looks ready to jump up and down in joy. "Bridget, I love you!"

Feeling someone's eyes on me, I turn around and see Darren standing at my elbow with raised brows.

"Hi," I say, the pitch of my voice unusually high.

"I like your sweater," he responds, his gaze taking in all of me.

"No you don't," I throw back.

Felipe clears his throat and asks, "Shot of *baijiu*, Boss?"

Darren shakes his head. Felipe moves to check on another customer.

"So let's take care of this egg-boiling lesson," Darren says.

I don't know why it didn't occur to me earlier, but if he really wanted to learn how to boil an egg, he could have asked his chef to teach him. My pulse quickens.

"Sure," I reply.

I follow him to what I think will be the kitchen, but instead we end up in front of an elevator.

"The kitchen's upstairs?" I ask, incredulous.

"Mine is, yes," he replies as he waits for me to step in first. "I live on the top floor."

"Oh."

We're going up to his place. I wonder if I should have said something to Amy, though the last I checked, she and JD were grinding on the dance floor. I step into the elevator.

"You're not warm in that thing?" Darren asks after the elevator doors close.

Well, now I am.

"My body runs cold," I explain. "I probably need to live in a place like Hawaii. Or Bali. My ex-boyfriend used to say, 'Cold hands, warm heart.'"

"Your ex go to Cal, too?"

I shake my head. "He went to Florida on a football scholarship. We tried the long-distance thing freshman year, but it was hard."

"So he's from the Bay Area."

"We both went to Oakland Tech."

"You ever try acupuncture to help with the cold hands?"

"I wouldn't mind giving it a try, but it's not exactly cheap, and it's not something student health services covers. That's a change in our medical system that I'd like to see: expanded coverage for wholistic care that draws on the best from all cultures."

"So you're pretty open-minded to things that go beyond the traditional?"

"Sure," I reply, though I wonder if he's referring to medicine only.

The elevator doors slide open. My heart accelerates. Is he expecting there to be more than just a lesson in boiling eggs? Do I hope that he wants more?

CHAPTER TWENTY-FOUR

DARREN

Past

I stand in front of the facial-recognition scanner to unlock my door.

"High tech," she comments as she follows me inside.

Her jaw drops.

The ceiling at my place is almost twenty feet high, floor-to-ceiling windows surround the great room, the flooring—Kempas hardwood imported from Malaysia—stretches the length, and the furnishings come mostly from Bentley Home or Brabbu.

"You can take off your sweater. I'll adjust the temperature so you won't get cold," I say, pulling a clothes hanger from the closet.

She slides off her sweater and hands it to me to hang up.

I look over her figure. "Nice dress."

"Thanks. It belongs to Simone. She lent me the jumpsuit I wore to the fundraiser."

Doesn't she have clothes of her own besides the sweater? I wonder.

Talking to my AI device, I give the instructions to turn up the thermostat two degrees.

"Drink?" I ask Bridget.

"Water would be great."

I show her into the kitchen, which is much larger than my needs, given that I don't cook.

I get a glass. "Still or sparkling?"

"Still. Sparkling makes me burp."

I put the glass into the filtered water dispenser.

"So where do you keep your pots?" she asks.

Does she really think I want a lesson on boiling eggs? Kimberly and I didn't even make it through dinner before we were tearing each other's clothes off. With this one, I have to take her grocery shopping and let her teach me how to boil eggs before making it to first base? Is she that oblivious?

But I open the cabinet door to show her the cookware.

"You have nice stuff," she says, taking out a pot. Looking it over, her eyes enlarge. "This is a Duparquet! I saw this on a cooking show once. A simple fry pan costs like four thousand dollars."

"I don't know a thing about cookware. Cheryl outfitted the kitchen for me."

Bridget shakes her head as she looks at the pot as if feeling sorry for it. "And you don't even cook."

I watch her fill the pot with water and notice her shoes don't go with her outfit. She'd make an incredible candidate for one of those makeover television programs. She's definitely the frumpiest thing to walk through my doors. Only she's not intrinsically frumpy. She just chooses to be.

"Last time you told me to put the eggs in first," I note.

"Right. Well, you can do the water first if you make sure you put the eggs in gently."

I open my refrigerator and pull out eggs. She takes two and puts them in the pot.

I wonder what my mother would think if I showed her Bridget.

"You want me to hang with a better crowd, how's this?" I imagine saying to her.

"You don't have to spend your time with JD just because you're his cousin," my mother had said to me on our call earlier. "You deserve better. And I heard the *Hei Long* is looking to start a war. A number of their top deputies were taken out, and they're looking for revenge."

"There's always talk about that," I had replied. The *Hei Long* is a triad based in Hong Kong.

"When it happens, I don't want you caught in it."

I've had this same conversation more than a dozen times. Once, I was so exasperated, I told her that if she wanted a normal life for her son, she should never have married a gangster in the first place.

"You should leave the *Jing San*, marry a nice girl, give me some adorable grandchildren," she had pouted.

"You coming to Andrea's wedding?" I had asked, switching the subject.

It worked. She talked about how it depends on how her aunt, who was recently discharged from the hospital, is doing, and how disappointed she is that her nephew, who lives closer to the aunt, is barely doing anything.

"You know Tony is no longer involved with the *Jing San*," my mother had informed me even though I already knew that about Tony. "He works with his brother now, making billions in legitimate business."

Spotting Bridget and Amy in the club then, and not wanting to rehash my mother's concerns, I had told her I needed to go.

"After the eggs are done, put them in cold water," Bridget tells me once the eggs are on the stove. "That way the yolk doesn't turn greenish-gray."

"The yolks turn green?" I ask.

"It has something to do with the heat affecting the iron and sulfur in the eggs."

"Never knew that about eggs."

"How long have you had this place?" Bridget asks as she looks around the kitchen again.

"About four years. You make your collard greens and sweet potato pie?"

"I was going to, but I'll do it tomorrow instead."

"You ever been to a restaurant called Maybelle's?"

Her eyes light up. "That place has *the best* sweet potato pie. The crust is made from scratch and it's to die for!"

The look on her face makes me wish I had a slice of Maybelle's pie right now.

"Dante used to take me there for my birthdays."

"Dante the ex?" I ask, even though I'm not keen to talk about her past boyfriends.

"Yeah. Does it ever get weird for you seeing your ex, Kimberly, with another guy?"

"Nope."

"I don't know what she sees in Eric Drumm."

I lean against the kitchen island. "Money, money, and more money. Maybe prestige if his dad becomes president."

She lifts a brow. "Think highly of your ex much?"

"I'm not knockin' her. I might date Drumm if I were her."

"You could do so much better. *She* could do so much better."

"She's the daughter of immigrants who worked as cooks in a Chinese restaurant, and she's probably reached the pinnacle of her modeling career. There's not a whole lot of places she can go in a few years. Marrying a Drumm is a huge step up for her."

"Well, I hope she's happy then."

"Really?" I ask with doubt.

"Really."

"After the way she's treated you?"

"You made me feel sorry for her."

I stare at Bridget. She, a woman whose high in life is driving a Honda Accord, feels sorry for Kimberly, a beautiful woman who, even if she doesn't end up marrying Drumm, will find some sugar daddy twice her age, and could very well live in the lap of luxury for the rest of her life? It makes no sense.

I'd better fuck her soon. I don't want her nonsense rubbing off on me.

"Don't," I tell her. "She'd never feel sorry for you."

Bridget tilts her head to one side as she studies at me. "So you dated her because…she's hot?"

"That's as good a reason as any, isn't it?"

"It's a good reason to have sex, but usually there's a little more going on for a relationship."

Deciding I need a drink, I ask. "You want something more than water? I'm gonna get myself a bourbon."

I walk out into living room and over to the bar. It's an open floor plan, so we can still hold a conversation while she remains in the kitchen.

"You a couples' therapist on the side?" I ask as I pour myself a shot.

"Just interested in people. Curious what kind of guy you are."

I down the shot. "You don't want to know."

"Now why would you say that?"

Not liking the way her gaze is boring into me, I pour myself another shot. I should have her leave. Find another Kimberly or an Olga to invite up to my place instead. I know what to do with women like that. I don't know what to do with a Bridget Moore.

"If I were a therapist, I'd say that kind of statement suggests self-esteem issues," she teases. "Either that or you're trying to be mysterious."

Glass of bourbon in hand, I walk back to her and stand close enough to catch a whiff of whatever shampoo she uses. What's a mystery is why I want to jump her bones right now.

As if sensing my thoughts, she takes a step back to put distance between us. But she bumps into the counter behind her.

"So what about you shouldn't I know?" she asks.

Putting the shot glass down on the counter behind her, I lean in and lower my voice. "I don't give a fuck about learning how to boil eggs."

Her lashes flutter quickly. It seems she wants to look away from me, but she's a deer caught in my headlights.

"Oh," was all she musters for a reply.

"And you don't either," I tell her.

She looks affronted. "Just because I came up here doesn't mean I—"

Cupping her jaw, I cut off her words with a kiss. Not a devouring one, but a firm, demanding one that gives her a glimpse of how much I want her.

She tastes good. She smells good. She feels good.

Incredibly so.

My ardor spikes. I want more, but I have to gauge her reception. When I pull away, her breath is uneven, her pupils dilated, her lips soft.

She doesn't look alarmed, but she's hesitant, as if she's trying to decide how she should respond. To help her make up her

189

mind, I press my lips to hers again. I'm gentle. Tender. Things I'm usually not.

Eventually her lips part to allow me to go deeper. I take my time, teasing her with my tongue. Her body relaxes. Cupping the back of her head near her neck, I work her mouth more. Heat roils in my groin. I delve deeper into her mouth.

God, this is good.

Weaving my fingers through her hair, I clasp her closer. Her hands fly up defensively and come to rest on my chest. I want to grind my hips into her, but I don't want to come off too aggressive. Instead, I kiss her harder, claiming her mouth, every inch of lips, palate, tongue. I take whole mouthfuls of her until she sounds breathless.

She tries to talk, but the words are muffled by my lips.

"The eggs," she finally manages when our lips unlock for a second.

I realize the eggs are banging against the pot. Leaning over, I turn off the stove, then promptly turn my attention back to her.

"We should—" she starts.

But my mouth covers hers again. This time I wrap an arm around her waist and press her to me. She can probably feel my hard-on against her belly, but she doesn't push me away. In fact, she's actively returning my kiss now. As much as she can, that is. I'm conducting this kiss. I position her head so that I can access her mouth from different angles. She exhales a soft moan when I move off her mouth to taste her neck and kiss my way to her shoulder.

A small warning goes off in the back of my head. I should

stop. It's not too late. But what's the worst that can happen? I get her out of my system, but she develops feelings for me and I have to break her heart.

Nevertheless, I pause. She seems to pick up on my hesitation.

"I never told Amy where I was going," she says. "What if she's looking for me?"

I doubt it.

As if on cue, I get a text from JD. After pulling out my cell and reading it, I show the text to Bridget.

Going back to my place with Amy.

"Oh," Bridget says, a little disconcerted. Maybe she feels like Amy abandoned her.

Which means she's alone here with me.

And all mine.

CHAPTER TWENTY-FIVE

BRIDGET

Past

I can't believe Amy abandoned me like that. Now what am I supposed to do?

I look up from his cellphone and back at Darren.

"Mind if I call her?" I ask him.

He calls JD and hands the phone to me.

"Hi, JD, it's Bridget," I say. "Can I talk to Amy?"

I step away from Darren. It was getting a little too hot and heavy for comfort.

"Hey, Bridget," Amy says. "The bartender said you were with Darren, so I figured it would be okay if I took off."

I walk out of the kitchen and into the living area for some privacy. "Well, I…"

"I would've texted you, but, you know, they took our phones."

"When will you be done?"

"I don't know. JD said he'll give me a ride back whenever. I'm sure Darren would do the same for you. Have fun!"

Before I can say anything, Amy hangs up. I hold on to the phone, trying to think what I should do next. This is my chance to leave if I want to. If he starts kissing me again, I doubt I'll have the fortitude to pull away. My body won't want to. And yet, I'm nervous about a guy who can make me orgasm with a simple foot rub.

Why does he want to kiss *me* anyway when he has models at his disposal? It's not that I think I'm unattractive, but I doubt I'm his type. Did JD put him up to it? Is he supposed to entertain me so that JD can make inroads with Amy? Not that he needs any assistance in that department. Maybe they made a bet, a challenge to see if Darren can seduce the nerdy-looking coed with the ugly sweater.

Feeling movement behind me, I turn around.

"Thanks for letting me use your phone," I stall, handing it back to him.

I'm about to ask him about his club's policy regarding cellphones when, instead of taking the phone, he takes my wrist and yanks me to him. The phone falls to the floor.

"Your phone—" I gasp.

But he cups my face between his hands, and his mouth is on mine, cutting off my words, taking my breath. I grasp both his forearms with my hands. Other than that, my body seems incapable of doing anything else except submitting to his kiss, which is heavier and more forceful than before. Currents go through me, warming me, melting my insides.

Eventually, one of his hands moves to my back, trapping me against him. I wasn't going anywhere anyway. My lips seem sealed to his. His kiss is so controlling. It's like I can't get a word in edgewise. He's the predator, and I'm what gets eaten. Only he isn't messy about it. He's not a horny teenager. He's a practiced artisan. I've never been kissed like this before.

A small part of me feels like this is a joke. Like someone's going to pop out from behind a camera to inform me I've been pranked on some reality TV show. That Darren won the bet about seducing me.

Screw it. I don't care if it *is* a bet. I should just enjoy this like I enjoyed that foot massage.

When Darren drops his hand from my back to my ass, I let him. My head swims with the onslaught of sensations, how he seems to fill all my senses, as if all around me, nothing but him exists.

Gripping the backs of my legs with both hands, he hoists me up to his waist and carries me to the sofa. He sits down. I like my position straddled over his lap, because it gives me more height with which to kiss him. My hands wrap his head, fingers entwining in his hair. Our kissing goes on and on, an urgency below my navel grows. His hands caress my back, cradle my neck, and hold my head in place whenever he wants to push his tongue deeper into my mouth.

Turning, he leans me down into the sofa until I'm completely beneath him. I like the weight of him upon me, but it's not the best position to be in if I decide I don't want to take things any further.

But I do. Or, at least, my body does. It's burning for him. *I'm* the horny teenager here. I groan when he licks and sucks the side of my neck, sigh when he kisses the soft spot beneath my jaw, and gasp when reaches beneath my dress. Running his hand up my thigh, he finds my underwear. It's damp. He continues to kiss the area about my neck and collar as his fingers caress me through the panties. The fabric rubs against my clit, and I whimper.

His mouth clamps back down on mine. I don't know what to focus on: his forceful devouring of my mouth or the delicious flutters between my legs. For several minutes, I vacillate between the two until the tension in my lower body takes precedence.

Shifting, he slips his hand down into my panties. His fingers connect with my flesh, stroking me, making me writhe. I haven't felt this wound up since…I have no memory at the moment. This is different from the foot massage, which went from relaxation to pleasure to orgasm. This is tension, yearning, even desperation. His fondling has me giddy with arousal, fearful that he might stop, and hot with need.

Lucky for me, he seems committed to the end. He drags his forefinger along my clit and makes circles with the soft, pliant nub. My back arches. He finds a spot more sensitive than the rest and digs in. My mouth drops.

Please, oh yes, please.

To my surprise, my climax looms over me already. I close my eyes to home in on the rapture awaiting me. The sweet heat of his fondling sends me to another space.

Minutes later, pleasure blossoms through my lower region. I quake and twitch beneath him.

He slows his caresses while he covers my mouth with his. My arousal still percolates, but I sigh with satisfaction against his lips. His fingers slip lower and curl into my slit. I gasp. He's found another spot that eagerly rears at the attention. It doesn't take much before I'm moaning and digging my fingers into his triceps; the most delicious agitation swells in me with each stroke of his.

"Oh, God," I plead in a small voice.

This orgasm is going to be more intense than the last, and I worry that I won't be able to control how my body reacts. He quickens his ministrations and kisses me harder. With a cry, muffled by his mouth, I lose it.

It's as if all the pressure in me has collapsed into the area between my legs before bursting all over. I buck and shake like I have epilepsy.

I'm not quite recovered when he pushes himself up and undoes the top two buttons of his shirt before pulling it off. He unbuckles his belt next.

"Wait, I didn't bring anything," I say. Maybe he'd be okay with a hand job?

He gets off the sofa, sweeps me up and tosses me over his shoulder. For a moment, I admonish myself for letting my guard down with someone I haven't known that long.

He carries me into his bedroom, which is just as spectacular as the rest of the residence. Dim recessed lighting turn on automatically the instant he walks through the door. The bed, swathed in white and slate bed linen, looks larger than king-sized. A wide fireplace faces the bed, and there's a huge skylight above to see the stars and night sky.

I'm dumped on the bed and know he's intent on taking his turn now. From a bedside drawer, he pulls out a condom. He puts it between his teeth so that he can undo his pants and pull them off. My gaze takes in his chiseled chest, tapered hips, and the bob of his erection. He's so sexy that even a condom in his mouth looks especially hot.

I guess we're going all the way.

Tearing open the wrapper, he unrolls the condom over his shaft. My pussy flutters in anticipation. But he doesn't shove it in yet. Instead, he takes off my shoes, pulls down my underwear, and caresses my legs before settling between them. He rubs the tip against me, teasing me until I start to feel hot and bothered again.

I raise my hips, an invitation he takes and pushes in. A vein in his neck pulses. Our gazes meet. His stare makes my pussy throb. He sinks in farther. I haven't had sex in a while, and he feels especially hard as he stretches me.

"Fuck, you feel good," he murmurs, pressing farther, until he's fully buried inside my wet heat.

He exhales. I clench down on his shaft, wanting more of him. He braces himself by putting his arms on either side of me, then slowly begins to roll his hips. It feels amazing. *He* feels amazing. My arousal is primed to take more of him.

He slides one arm beneath my leg, opening me further so that he can thrust deeper.

"Oh, God," I find myself pleading again. I grasp the arm still braced near me.

The pace and pressure is perfect. Once in a while, I yelp when he shoves a little too hard, but mostly the push and pull of his cock, the grinding of his pelvis against my clit casts me on a wave of delight, enticing my appetite for more. I've never come three times in a row before. Twice, yes. But three is exciting.

He straightens and fondles my clit with his thumb. This shoots me over the edge. I grab the bedcover beneath me as I quake and cry. My pussy pulses madly.

Wow.

When I emerge from the rapture, I feel relaxed and invigorated at the same time. Darren rolls me on top of him. I straddle his pelvis and try to repay the favor. He gropes my breasts through the dress as I ride him, working up a small sweat. I should have taken off Simone's dress, but I'll make sure I wash it before I give it back. He grabs my hips and helps me grind myself into him.

"Oh, fuck, yeah," he mutters, bucking his hips up at me.

We're both perspiring from the exertion.

"Want to come again, Bridge?" he asks.

Seriously? A fourth time?

"I don't have to," I murmur, wanting him to have a turn.

"Rhetorical question," he replies as he insinuates his thumb between where our bodies are joined and rubs my clit.

I *love* the stimulation of my clit while filled with him. In my opinion, it's the most perfect pairing. Better than chocolate and peanut butter, or macaroni and cheese. Anything.

"You're going to come for me no matter what."

No matter what? Like I have no choice?

But my desire is headed toward that boiling point. Again. He works my clit like he owns it. And I let him. Because I don't want to deny my body just to make a show of my free will.

"That's it," he says, flexing his cock inside me.

His other hand is still on my hip, and he rocks me over his pelvis. I come undone. If he weren't holding on to me, I'd probably spasm right off him. My body strains against his continued fondling of my clit till he finally backs off. I collapse onto his chest, stunned that I was able to come again.

Before I can fully bask in the afterglow, he flips me off and onto my stomach, pulls my dress up and penetrates me from behind. This time, he thrusts harder, but somehow I can take it better from this position.

His erection stimulates a new part of me, and after a while, the prospect of a fifth climax greets me.

He varies his movements between gentle bucking and hard slamming, sometimes pulling himself all the way out. I whine at the emptiness till he shoves himself back in with enough force to make my teeth chatter. I'm desperate enough by now not to mind, though I do try to angle myself to soften the blows a little. There's not much I can do, however, but lie there, my fingers entangled with the bed linen, and submit to his fucking.

He slows enough for me to fix on my impending orgasm. His motions feel so incredible. A few strokes at just the right angle, and shudders rack my body.

This climax is the most amazing so far. My whole body is drowning in it. Even my screams are lost in the wave of ecstasy until the peak passes, and I realize how hard Darren is pounding me. His roar joins my cries as he reaches his finish. After several forceful pumps, he withdraws and falls onto the bed beside me.

The area between my thighs still pulses, sending ripples down my legs. Eyes closed, I lay quietly and listen to the sound of his breathing return to normal. My mind is devoid of thought, and before I know it, I've drifted off to sleep.

*****

When I wake, early morning light streams through the window. I'm definitely not in my own bed because my bedcover and sheets don't feel nearly this soft. Realizing I'm still at Darren's place, I sit up. I can't believe I've slept the whole night here. I was expecting to get sent home after we were done with the sex.

"Sorry, I forgot to shut the blinds," Darren says.

Turning, I find him sitting in the seating area in front of the window. He wears only pajama pants, and I drink in his upper body: the muscles of his arms, the chiseled chest, the six-pack. Unconsciously, I lick my lips.

"Breakfast?" he asks.

On the table beside him is a tray with a glass of juice, an individual French press, toast, and…boiled eggs?

Peeling back the bed covers, I slide out of bed and take the lounge chair opposite him. "Did you make all this?"

"I'm not completely inept." He pours the coffee into a cup.

I take the cup and add cream and a little sugar. "Thanks."

"I wasn't sure what kind of coffee you liked, so I picked a medium roast."

"Honestly, I don't know the difference between the different types of coffee. Most times, we just have instant coffee in our apartment."

I take a sip. So this is what really good coffee tastes like.

"You make the eggs, too?" I ask.

"Per your instructions."

I set down the coffee and reach for one of the egg cups. I tap the shell with the butter knife to crack it, cut off the top and marvel that the egg yolk is a perfect bright yellow, not even a hint of ring around it.

"I learn quick," Darren supplies.

"Yeah," I second. "I'm impressed. You gonna have any breakfast?"

"I already ate."

I like the way he looks in the morning, his hair a little tossed instead of perfectly gelled back.

"What time is it?" I ask before biting into the toast.

"Just before nine."

I start. "I'm supposed to meet with my study group at ten-thirty!"

In my head, I go over how fast I can get myself out of here, back to my apartment to change and grab my textbook and notes, and make it over to Moffitt Library.

"I'll give you a lift," Darren offers before heading to his walk-in closet to dress.

"Thanks," I sigh in relief. I would be hard-pressed to make it taking public transportation. I quickly finish the egg and take a few gulps of the coffee before looking around for my underwear. Spotting it on the floor, I slip in on and try not to relive all that happened last night.

"There're extra toothbrushes in the bathroom," Darren informs me.

I can't help but wonder how often he has women over if he keeps spare toothbrushes around.

Like the rest of the place, the bathroom is stunning. It also has a large skylight above. The fixtures and lighting look like they were polished yesterday. The shower looks like it's built for four or five people—who needs such a large shower? On the other side of the feature wall is a rectangular Jacuzzi bathtub wrapped in granite. I stand on a furry bathmat before the sink and unwrap a new toothbrush.

Did I really have five orgasms last night? Counting the foot rub, that makes six total orgasms. That's more than I have in a month most times.

When I'm done with the bathroom, and have tried to make my hair look less messy by using my fingers as a comb, I step out and see that Darren, dressed in sweats and a muscle tank, looks as hot as ever.

"Your cell's on the table," he tells me. "I had security bring it up."

I go get my phone so that I can text my classmates that I'll likely be a little late. I then send a text to Amy to see how she's doing.

Darren's fairly quiet as we take the elevator down to the parking garage. I wonder if he regrets what happened last night.

"Thanks for breakfast," I say after we're in his Panamera. I think about offering him some of the sweet potato pie that I plan on making, but I don't know if he would even care for it. Plus, that would entail us meeting again, and I'm not sure if he wants that either.

So I decide to talk about his club instead. "How long have you been the owner of The Lotus?"

"I started it four years ago," he answers.

"What made you decide to open a club?"

"I had family who liked to hang out at the Crimson Dragon Restaurant before it burned down. I decided to provide a replacement, but one less stuffy and old school."

"You have a lot of family here in San Francisco?"

"Extended family."

"That must be nice. I wish I knew who my extended family were."

Neither one of us is particularly chatty on the ride back to Berkeley. As he pulls up in front of my apartment, I wonder what I should say in parting. See you around? Thank you for the amazing orgasms?

His cell rings. The call goes through to the car.

"I need to talk. You clear?" the man on the other end asks.

"Not yet," Darren replies.

I check the time and turn to him. "I should hurry. Thanks for the ride."

He nods and turns back to his call.

I walk up to the building and turn around to wave just before going inside, but I can't tell through the dark tint of his car windows if he sees me.

Once inside, I let out a long breath. Well, that wasn't much of a goodbye. After the sex we had, if he was interested in more than that, we would have at least exchanged a peck on the cheek, right? At least he personally drove me home. He could have sent me off in a taxi or had one of his staff members drive me back. And it was nice of him to make breakfast. He didn't have to do that.

Still, I have a feeling I probably won't ever see him again.

CHAPTER TWENTY-SIX

DARREN

Past

I watch Bridget wave at me before she goes inside her apartment building.

It's better that I didn't kiss her goodbye. I could tell she was wondering if I would. But I didn't want to give her the impression that we'd see each other again. I got what I needed last night.

Sort of.

"Hey, Darren, you there?" asks Ray.

"Yeah," I respond.

"I got a tip from my inside man at Customs that they're going to do a major inspection of all ships originating in Fujian. JD's not picking up his phone, but I thought he might want to know ASAP."

"His current shipment isn't due for a week, I think, but I'll let him know."

After hanging up with Ray, I sent JD a message to call me. And to quell any lingering desire I have for Bridget, I put myself through an extra-hard workout at the gym. I go through several intervals, mixing high-intensity cardio with weightlifting.

But as I cool down on the bike, my mind wanders back to the night before, back to how she felt, how she smelled, how she tasted. And how she came. Picturing her with her mouth wide open, her body shaking from head to toe, I start to get a boner.

What would her orgasms look like after a little BDSM? Would she go for some flogging? How would she take bastinado? I bet a pair of nipple clamps would look great on her.

Fuck.

Maybe I didn't bang her hard enough. I held back because I wasn't sure what she could handle. Not sure why I cared, if I didn't plan to see her again.

Her body was surprisingly responsive. I counted five orgasms. Usually it takes a little longer for me to figure out a woman's go-to triggers. Guess I got lucky with Bridget. As the saying goes, first time's the charm. Only it rarely ever is the case. Especially in sex.

"What's up?" JD asks when he calls me back.

Before responding, I check that the encryption app on my phone is working. Developed by Golden Technologies, founded by one of the legitimate Lee family members, it scrambles phone calls in case our line is tapped.

"Got a tip from Ray," I reply. "Customs is cracking down. You might want to rethink your current shipment."

"Shit. All right. Hey, I told Amy she could meet me at your club tonight. I told her to just bring herself this time. Figure you've babysat her friend enough."

To my surprise, I greet this with mixed feelings.

*****

Bridget has invaded my thoughts every damn day for the past six days since I saw her last. I actually thought about calling her, especially last night when JD brought Amy to the club again for the umpteenth time. I would have enjoyed my time with Bridget over listening to Manny talk about how great his meeting with Tran went and how they're set to open two massage parlors in one suburban downtown in the East Bay.

"We just need more women to work the parlors," Manny told me. "I talked to Henry, but he's one of those old farts who don't like the PSB. In fact, he's so old, he could die any day, right? He must be grooming someone to take over. You know who that is?"

I reminded Manny that I just offer a safe place for members and friends to congregate. I don't get into the logistics of the different branches of triad business, especially activities related to sex trafficking. My mother constantly urges the less I know, the better.

It's early evening, and I make my way over to the other side of The Lotus to see who's around. It looks kind of slow tonight, but there are two women playing openly on the main floor.

I sit down on a chair to watch.

The busty blond, wearing a leather dominatrix outfit, has her naked submissive on all fours and tied to an oversized ottoman. I'd like to see Bridget in that position.

The Domme circles a flogger against the sub's ass. With Bridget, I'd start with something simple, like a gentle flogging.

After warming up her sub, the Domme snaps the tips of the tails against her sub. The latter yelps, but it shouldn't hurt too badly. I wonder what Bridget's pain tolerance is.

Next, the blond attaches a strap-on to herself, stands before her sub, and presents the black rubber dildo. Her sub eagerly takes it in. Again, I picture Bridget in the sub's place. Warmth swirls in my groin.

Withdrawing, the Domme goes down on one knee to lock lips with her sub. After a long, wet kiss, she gets up and goes to stand behind her sub. She positions the dildo between the sub's legs and sinks in.

The sub moans. "Thank you, Mistress."

"You're my little cock whore, aren't you?" asks the Domme, shoving her hips at the sub.

"Yes, Mistress."

I watch with half a mind. The other half is thinking back to my night with Bridget, recalling how she looked, sounded, felt, tasted.

This isn't helping.

Getting up, I decide to go into my office and make a call to Benjamin Lee, a developer who's close to Tony. After talking with Ben about Drumm, I get a call from Lee Hao Young, who wants to stop by before he heads down to Los Angeles.

"It's nice to finally meet you, Darren," Hao Young, a short man with thinning hair, says as he sits down at the bar. He looks around. "Nice place you've built."

"Thanks. Something to drink?" I ask, playing bartender.

"I only drink green tea. Much better for health."

I motion to Grace, Cheryl's assistant, who usually comes in early.

"I've heard good things about you, Darren. Of course, your father was an exceptional man."

I tell Grace to get some tea for Hao Young before replying to him. "I hope you had a good trip here."

"I always enjoy coming to San Francisco. Such a beautiful city. Reminds me of my hometown of Chongqing. Have you been back to China?"

"A few times but never to Chongqing."

"JD is going in a few months. Perhaps you want to join him. Your cousin has a lot of promise. I see many opportunities for him."

"I'm good here."

"Has JD told you about his newer ventures?"

"I mind my own business."

"But he's your cousin."

I lean on the counter. "I appreciate your words, but I'm not looking to follow in my father's footsteps. Given how things turned out for him, I think you understand."

"Then who will take up his legacy? We, of course, will respect your decision, and are grateful for the role you have in the organization. But we need someone to step up and take over the counterfeiting division. This club of yours is nice, but it's—what do the Americans like to say?—little potatoes."

I remain quiet. On one shoulder is my mother, shaking her head.

"Your father sacrificed himself for the organization," Hao Young continues. "Now the organization is repaying the favor by granting you, his son, the opportunity of a lifetime. Don't you want to expand your horizons? This club cannot be challenging enough for someone like you."

It wasn't particularly challenging anymore, I have to admit. There wasn't another level I could take the success of the club. I've toyed with the idea of opening a restaurant, but it's not a passion of mine.

"Think about it," Hao Young says. "I know what your father would want you to do. And I hope that you will see this invitation with gratitude."

Grace returns with the tea, and our conversation turns to more mundane matters.

The club opens just as Hao Young departs. The first patron in the door is Manny, dressed in black slacks, a dark gray shirt, and a black blazer.

"Who was that?" Manny asks.

"Lee Hao Young."

"No way! What's he here for?"

"Business with JD."

Manny presses his lips together. "What kind of business?"

I shrug.

Manny's brow furrows in thought. "Why does JD get all the top opportunities? I'm just as good as he is."

One of Manny's favorite topics is griping about JD. I've heard it all before, so I make my way up the stairs.

Manny follows me. "I mean, I know he's your cousin, but wouldn't you agree? Just 'cause I don't have a fancy degree from UCLA doesn't mean I'm not a good businessman."

"Take it up with Hao Young," I suggest as I sit down. "He'll be back through San Francisco when he's done with LA."

"I will. Maybe after I get things going with Tran. Then they'll see that I'm a real asset. Better than JD."

"Better than me at what?"

Manny whips around to face JD.

"Nothing," he mutters as he brushes past JD and heads down the stairs.

"Manny jealous again?" JD asks me.

"Yeah," I answer. "He saw Lee Hao Young walk out."

"I don't know why we don't just dump Manny's ass."

"Cut him some slack. He just wants to be like you."

JD snorts. "He can wear all the Gucci suits he wants, he'll never be me. Anyway, Drumm and Kimberly are here. They should be up any minute."

"About Drumm. We should talk."

Before I can say anything more, I see Drumm coming up the stairs.

"Jesus, it's freezing out there," Drumm says. "Where the hell's the sunny California weather?"

"People confuse Northern California with Southern

California," JD replies. "We're in between the sunny beaches and the Pacific Northwest."

"You should all come out to Florida. We're the Sunshine State for a reason. So you guys in on the resort?"

"One of our good friends is in construction. You think you can hook him up on this project?"

"'Course I can," Eric says. "I get to call all the shots. I'll work your friend in."

I narrow my eyes. "Don't you want to know the company's credentials first?"

"If JD vouches for 'em, that's good enough for me."

I know the construction company JD is referring to. They've only landed a few smaller projects, nothing on par with a Drumm resort, and most of which were related to residential parking structures. Either Eric is shining JD on, or he's not a careful businessman.

"Your family doesn't seem to work with the larger construction companies," I say. "Why is that?"

Eric grins. "We like to give the little guys a chance."

"It's not because they're easier to push around?" I challenge, ignoring JD's stare. "There are over a dozen lawsuits from firms you've contracted with who say they haven't been paid the full amount for their work."

Eric frowns. "That's the problem with some of these little guys. Some of them do shoddy work."

"So why not go with the reputable companies?"

"Because...because most of them overcharge."

"Quality usually costs more."

Eric looks consternated.

"I'm not saying the larger construction firms are better," I continue, "but you guys have contracted with different companies for all your projects. You must have come across some smaller guys who are reliable and do good work. Why not work with them again?"

"We do work with the good ones again."

"Not according to Ben Lee."

"Ben doesn't know shit about how we run our business."

At that moment, Kimberly shows up, wearing a skin-tight leather jumpsuit and stiletto heels. Walking up to Eric, she gives him a kiss.

"Wow," Eric says with obvious admiration as he looks her over.

"You like it?" she asks, turning around to give him the 360.

JD rolls his eyes. He thumps me on the chest. "Ray's here. Let's go say hi. We'll be back."

Kimberly smirks at me as I follow JD.

"What's wrong with you?" JD asks as we make our way down the stairs. "You're acting like Amy's friend."

"I spoke with Ben Lee," I reply. "He said, 'You don't want to do business with a Drumm.'"

"Yeah, but we're not in this for business exactly. We're doing him a favor so that we can cash in on a favor when we need it."

"But the way they do business suggests they only look out for themselves. When we need their help, they'll help us out if it's in their *interest* to help us out. If not, we're shit out of luck. They've got no ethics."

JD stops and stares at me, agog. "Since when do we give a fuck about *ethics*? You forget we're gangsters?"

"We've still got to know what we're dealing with. And I don't trust Drumm."

"Why not? Eric's dad is like the ultimate gangster. He likes to run his business and the government like the fucking Godfather. We can relate, right?"

"I'm not looking to pay homage to Drumm."

"I don't get what your problem with Drumm is."

Sensing that I'm not going to persuade JD on Drumm's character faults, I say, "I want a return of some kind. Otherwise, there's better things I can do with my money."

Now JD looks consternated. "You sore because Drumm's dating your ex? Is that what this is?"

I don't even want to bother answering that question, even though I'm sure if I snapped my fingers, Kimberly would be back at my side.

"JD!"

We turn around and see Amy waving at us.

"Thank God," JD exhales and whispers to me, "I thought she was going to bring her friend this time because she said she felt bad coming here a lot without her, but I do not need that friend of hers here. Bad enough *you're* getting up in Drumm's face."

JD walks over to Amy. After I nod hello to her, I decide to get a drink from Felipe.

"Hey, Boss," Felipe greets. "Shot of Martin Mills?"

I raise my brows. "Where'd you get that?"

"You're not the only one with connections." Felipe pours a couple ounces. "Everything okay?"

It's too cliché to pour out my troubles to the bartender, so I take the whiskey and reply, "Yeah."

For some reason, the person I feel like talking to is Bridget. She'd understand my qualms regarding Drumm. It's too bad she didn't come with Amy tonight. Maybe I should give her a call.

"That's incredible," I say to Felipe of the complex butterscotch notes in the drink. "Thank you."

I walk back upstairs, where JD and Amy are now situated. I sit down opposite Amy. "You didn't bring Bridget with you."

She looks surprised. "Was I supposed to?"

"Hell no," JD replies before turning to a server. "Mojito for the lady. Extra mint."

"I'm with JD on that one," says Kimberly. "Talk about a downer. No offense, Amy, but where did you find her?"

"She's my friend," Amy replies, a little hurt. "And she's actually really nice. Though, I guess she can come across a little salty."

"A little?" Kimberly replies, exchanging a look of agreement with Eric.

"She speaks her mind," I say. I turn to Eric. "Like your dad."

"She's better off *not* speaking her mind," Kimberly says.

Eric chuckles. "Burn!"

"What are you, in the third grade?" I shoot back.

Surprised, Eric turns to JD. But I don't stick around to see who's side JD takes. I walk away to find Cheryl.

"I want the cell number for Bridget Moore," I tell her.

CHAPTER TWENTY-SEVEN

BRIDGET

Past

My cellphone rings, but it's a blocked number, so I let it go to voicemail. I'm already on the line with Aunt Coretta, whom I talk with at least once a month.

"You know you can spend spring break here in Denver with us," she tells me over the phone.

"I'd love to," I say as I grab a La Croix from the refrigerator and walk back to my room, "but I might need the time to catch up on stuff."

The truth is, the plane ticket is a little more than I can afford right now.

"Okay, I understand, Bridget honey. You know, I'd also understand if you couldn't make it out here for other reasons, too."

"Other reasons?"

"Like maybe a boy in your life?"

"No, it's school and my internship," I assure her as I pull on a zipper hoodie over my tank top and sweats before sitting down in front of my computer. The blocked number comes up again, but I decline the call.

"So there's no one in your love life? Anyone even on the radar?" asks Coretta.

For a second, Darren flashes through my head. But he and I haven't been in touch since the night at his place. As part of me suspected, it turned out to be a one-night stand. I don't regret it, though. It was the most amazing sex I've ever had. Not that I've had much sex to compare it to. I dated Dante for eight months and briefly dated a classmate last year for all of three months.

"Nope," I tell Coretta, "which works for me because I'm thinking to do an honors thesis. Maybe get a second job."

"That sounds like a lot. You do anything for fun?"

"Made your collard greens last weekend."

"That's the most fun you've had this week?"

I laugh, a little nervously, because I'm not about to confess to sex with Darren. Not to a woman I consider my second grandmother. "My friends and I hung out. Last night, Simone and I binge-watched half of season five of *The Wire*."

"That the one with Lance Reddick?"

"Yep."

"Oh, he's yummy."

I laugh. "Yeah, he is."

After we finish our conversation, Simone pops her head into my room. "You wanna watch a few more episodes tonight?"

"Sure. After I get an outline done for my Health Policy class."

I turn on my computer, glad that I'm not out at The Lotus

with Amy. Well, kind of glad. She's been to the club a few times this week already and is headed there again tonight. Now that she gets picked up by JD's driver and doesn't have to come back late on public transportation, there's less of a need to have an accompaniment.

"It's okay if I'm not invited," I had replied. "I've got a paper due in my Health Policy class."

"Cool."

A part of me was a little bummed not to be joining Amy for the chance to see Darren again, but it was best I get on with my normal life. Of course, I could have reached out to Darren myself and left him a message at his club. I'm not one of those old-fashioned women who believes the guy has to make all the moves. It's the vibe that I picked up from him when he dropped me home last weekend. If he wanted to see me again, he'd find a way to reach me. He could get my number from Amy via JD.

So if Darren wasn't interested, I wasn't going to pester him.

I try to review the article I need for my paper, but once Darren enters my mind, it's hard getting him out. My body wants to relive that night with him, and no amount of masturbating seems to do the trick.

"Aaargh," I growl at my desires. It must be that time of month when my hormones want my body to make a baby or something.

For the past 5 weeks (January 20-February 24), the CECC has rapidly produced and implemented a list of at least 124 action items, I read from the *Journal of the American Medical Association.*

I wonder what Darren's doing right now. Or who he's with.

Some other hot model like his ex? Actually, I wouldn't be surprised if Darren ended up back with Kimberly. If she had the choice, I can't see how she chooses Eric Drumm over someone like Darren. So what if Drumm has more money? Once you reach a certain threshold, does all that additional cash make a difference?

And there's no way Eric can be better in bed. I'm convinced that guys like Eric are too self-absorbed and arrogant to become good lovers.

Now, would Darren really choose to go back to Kimberly? Why not? There are guys whose insecurities require them to have eye candy on their arms to present to the world, guys who simply value looks over anything else.

I'm supposed to be analyzing health policy, not Darren's dating life. I go back to reading. *For the past 5 weeks (January 20-February 24), the CECC...*

Wait. I've read this already.

"I've got it," Simone tells me after a knock at the door.

It's probably Kat. She's always forgetting her keys at her boyfriend's place.

How did Coretta know to ask about my love life? She doesn't usually pry. We talk a lot about her grandchildren, the reason she moved out to Denver, and reminisce about her days in Oakland. Maybe it's something in the air.

I go back to the article. *For the past 5 weeks...*

"Hey."

The voice startles me because I recognize it, and it's not whom I expected.

Glancing toward my door, I see Darren, looking super-hot in a casual blazer over a white oxford and chinos.

"What are you doing here?" I ask.

"You greet everyone like that?" he returns.

I flush. "I mean, hi. But seriously, what are you doing here?"

"You didn't come to the club with Amy."

Because I wasn't invited. Instead, I say, "Oh, um, I have a paper I need to work on."

"Yeah? When's it due?"

"Next Friday."

"So you could have come tonight."

"Yeah, well, I wanted to get a head start on the paper. Plus, I told Simone we'd camp out in front of the TV together tonight."

At that moment, Simone passes by my room on the way to hers. "We can catch *The Wire* another time." She turns to Darren. "Nice meeting you."

He nods. When he turns back to me, Simone, standing behind him, points at him, then fans herself as if she's overheating. With a wink, she turns to leave.

I blush deeper.

"Something the matter?" Darren asks.

I shake my head. "No! I just—you didn't say why you're here?"

"Like I said, you weren't at the club. And I tried calling you, but you didn't pick up."

"Oh. Were you expecting me at The Lotus tonight?"

"I didn't have any expectations one way or another. Probably better you didn't come. Your two favorite people, Kimberly and Eric Drumm, were there tonight."

"Yeah, definitely better I'm not there," I say with exaggerated sentiment.

He laughs as he walks into the room and removes his blazer. I eye the muscles in his arms and the way his shirt fits his body.

"Well, I pulled a Bridget Moore on Eric Drumm tonight," he says, sitting down on my bed.

"Really? I'm sorry I missed that. What happened?"

"I started asking him about why the Drumms rarely ever contract with the same company twice, why they never go with the larger, more well-known construction firms."

"Because it's easier to bully smaller firms."

"And you're right: even though they talk about cracking down on immigration, a lot of the companies the Drumms use hire illegal immigrants."

I can't help but beam.

As if wanting to put the brakes on my enthusiasm, he adds, "Before you go signing me up as some kind of progressive, I don't care about his immigration policy. What I don't like is how Drumm says one thing but then acts differently."

"They're hypocrites."

"JD doesn't see it. Or maybe he just doesn't care."

"It amazes me how many people are like that when it's so obvious to me that the Drumms lack a moral compass. They don't care about anyone except themselves. They'll help others as long as it suits their own purposes."

"I don't have a moral compass, but I have principles: one of them being that I don't deal with douchebags."

"That sounds like a good principle to me." I look at him quizzically. "Why don't you think you have a moral compass?"

He leans back against the wall and thinks. "Because I don't do the kind of crap that makes the world a better place."

"First of all, making the world a better place isn't 'crap,' and just because you aren't proactive in something doesn't mean you're a bad person. You don't have to be a saint to have a moral compass."

But he doesn't seem to want to talk about it. Staring at me, he says, "Come here."

My pulse quickens immediately. Looking at him, I feel like a mouse about to go after cheese, only it's part of a trap, and I'm about to be devoured.

"Why?" I ask. I put in a lot of effort this past week to forget about him, now all that's going to be for nothing.

"Because I said so."

I almost laugh, but then realize he's serious. He can't expect me to obey because he "said so." Only I do. I reason to myself that I'm simply picking my battles and because I'm curious.

Tentatively, I rise from my chair and sit down on the bed next to him. His gaze follows me the whole time like he's a panther stalking its prey.

He doesn't say anything right away, and I'm about to call him on his staring, but I'm not fast enough. His hand is at the back of my neck and his lips are on mine.

The trap is sprung, and I can't escape. I don't *want* to escape. What I want is to melt and thrill to his kiss. He claims every part of my mouth, more roughly than before. My senses reel at the force of his kiss, his nearness, his scent.

I hear a noise from Simone's room and manage to disengage myself. "My roommate's here."

"So? She's an adult."

"But…"

Darren rises and goes over to close the door. I gulp. Closing the door means he intends to do more kissing, and maybe more than kissing. I'm okay with kissing, but I don't want to have sex with my roommate just a few yards away. Amy once had a guy over last year on a weekend when I was away. Simone had been furious with all the noise they'd made.

"This is an old building," I explain. "The walls are thin."

"So we'll be quiet."

I also don't want to have to get over him all over again. Hopping off the bed, I try to buy myself time to sort out what I should do. "You want something to drink first?"

Before I can reach the door, however, he catches me and pins me to the wall. He looks down at me, daring me not to want this.

He answers slowly. "No, I don't want a drink first."

Locked in his gaze, my body buzzing, I don't think I want a drink, either. He waits a beat; it's my chance to object. When I don't, he smothers my mouth with his. Desire leaps within me, swirling me in its maelstrom. Damn hormones.

He presses his body to mine, sandwiching me between two hard planes. Cupping my face in both hands, he delves into my mouth, burning away my resistance. Briefly, I wonder if Simone heard the thump of my body against the wall and half expect her to knock on my door to make sure everything is okay. As Darren's tongue entwines with mine, I cease to care. I'm going to enjoy this kiss and hope that I have the wherewithal to stop things before we go any further.

After several minutes of intense face sucking, he shoves his hand down my sweats and into my underpants.

"You're soaking wet," he observes.

I tend to get wet easily, but with Darren, I feel like he's turned on a faucet. Even the way he stares into my eyes, like he's doing now, has me all riled up inside. He watches my face as he slowly fondles me, taking in my parted lips, my furrowed brow and fluttering lashes.

I should put a stop to this now before my arousal is fully in the driver's seat.

But it feels too good. Way too good.

I try to suppress my groans and gasps, keeping them to soft grunts and whispered moans. He rubs and teases my clit till I'm crazy with need. His fingers spread my moisture over my flesh, and my body just keeps pouring it on.

Darren notices, too. "You always get this wet, or is this just for me?"

I don't want to inflate his ego, but when I meet his gaze, my eyes give it away.

Lowering his head, he whispers into my ear, "Good answer."

He intensifies his masturbation until I erupt in small spasms, gasping loudly till I remember about my housemate.

He puts his forehead to mine. "That feel good?"

A quiver zips through me. I exhale a shaky breath. "Yeah."

Pulling away from me, he undoes his pants. I reach for his erection and stroke it.

"You're wet, too," I say of the precum.

Bracing one arm beside me, he pushes me into the wall again with his body, then catches my mouth with his, smothering and overwhelming me with his lips and tongue. I fondle his cock, hoping to return the favor and get him off. But he picks me up and deposits me on the bed. I can see in his eyes that a hand job isn't going to suffice. He wants more.

CHAPTER TWENTY-EIGHT

DARREN

Past

Bridget's eyes widen with worry. About that housemate of hers, I think.

"You have any health issues?" I ask her as I whip out a condom and tear open the wrapper.

The question puzzles her, but she answers, "No, but the walls here are thin—"

I roll the condom on. "You've said that."

Tentatively, she stares at my cock. A part of her wants it.

I grab her sweats. She tries to wiggle away, but I yank them down.

"Seriously!" she yelps.

Grabbing her legs, I pull her down to the foot of the bed, where I am. My pants have settled near my ankles, allowing me to kneel between her thighs.

"Don't worry, I've got it," I assure her as I position my cock at her sweet, wet slit.

"How—?"

Laying my body over hers, I clamp my hand over her mouth

and nose, then sink into her with my cock. She grunts against my hand as I push my entire length into her. She feels incredible. It would be even more amazing without the condom.

Imagining what that would be like spikes my arousal. I have to take a long breath to calm my desire to pound into her like there's no tomorrow.

Slowly, I withdraw, then sink back in. I keep my gaze on her face. She grabs my wrist with both hands and lightly tugs. She murmurs. I rock my hips, lightly thrusting into her. Her grip tightens and she pulls harder. I let my hand slide off her nose, giving her a chance to breathe as I buck deeper. Damn, her cunt feels so good.

"Want to try it again?" I ask.

She doesn't respond.

My hand, still covering her mouth, would have muffled her answer, but since she didn't shake her head, I pinch her nose between my thumb and forefinger. After several seconds, she yanks on my arm. Her body tries to buck me off, but I pump my hips faster and harder.

When she digs her fingernails into me, I release her nose. She starts to pant.

"Take it easy," I tell her to stall her hyperventilation.

She focuses on her breath and evens her breathing. Her eyes are luminous. I don't think I've ever used that word before. Tenderly, I brush away a tendril from her face as I find an angle and pace that she seems to like.

"You're going to come for me," I tell her. "Nice and hard."

Still holding my wrist with both hands, she meets my thrusts and grinds her hips at me.

"One more time," I say, covering her nose again.

This time, I cut off her air longer. Her body twitches and writhes like crazy beneath me. I quell the pressure to blow my load.

She's trying her best to yank my hand away. Panic creeps into her eyes. I drop my hand. She sucks in oxygen through her mouth.

Just before she cries out, I clasp my hand back over her mouth and watch as she comes, her fingers digging into me, her body shaking, her eyes rolling toward the back of her head. I pump long and hard for my own release. Swallowing my own groan, I tremble as euphoria surges through me. It feels fucking *amazing*.

At the same time, I know it can feel even more incredible.

I want this. Every day.

Her pussy pulses madly about my cock, which throbs for a while before finally settling down. I pull out and sit beside her, practically falling off the side of her tiny bed.

"How was it?" I ask, taking off the condom.

She stares up at the ceiling. Then, turning to me, she grabs her pillow and slams it against me. "You scared the hell out of me!"

"Your first time with breath play?" I inquire.

"Breath what?"

Standing, I pull my pants up and stare at her. "How was your orgasm?"

She bristles. "Intense."

I grin to myself. "It's called breath play."

She looks askance in thought.

"Was it quiet enough for you?" I ask.

Her face is already flushed, but her blush deepens, making her even prettier.

I watch her pull her sweats back up. "What are you doing next weekend?" The words are out of my mouth before I have a chance to really think about them.

"Nothing in particular," she replies. "I have an exam to study for in my statistics class."

"Want to go to Phuket?"

"Um, okay."

I shrug into my jacket. "We'll apply for your visa first thing tomorrow. You have your passport?"

"Passport? Phuket's a restaurant, right?"

I laugh. "Not the Phuket I'm referring to."

She stares at me agog, then narrows her eyes, probably thinking that I'm joking. "No, I can't go to Phuket. I don't have a passport."

I think through whom I know who could expedite a passport for me, or at least get me a counterfeit one. I'll talk to Cheryl.

"I'll see what I can do," I say and open the bedroom door.

She follows me into the hall. "You're not serious?"

I shouldn't be. This is one of the strangest things I've ever done. There are a dozen women I could take to Andrea's wedding who would make more sense than Bridget Moore. I stop at the threshold and look her over in her hoodie and sweats. Suspecting she doesn't have a wardrobe for the occasion, I say, "You'll need to go shopping."

She continues to look puzzled and in doubt.

I cup her jaw, tilt her chin, and claim her mouth, not for a goodbye kiss but a thorough tasting. Reluctantly, I manage to separate myself before my desire heats up too much.

"I'll call you tomorrow," I tell her, then open the door.

She stares after me as I descend the stairs. It feels strange having asked Bridget Moore to the wedding, but I actually can't think of anyone else who would be better. She'll be a fish out of water among the wedding guests, but Cheryl's attending the wedding, so I'll enlist her aid in making Bridget presentable.

I walk out of the building and breathe in the crisp night air. The more I think about spending time with Bridget, the less strange it feels. In fact, it feels good.

It feels…right.

Excerpt

CLAIMED HARDER

CHAPTER ONE

DARREN

Present

Coming inside of Bridget felt *intense*—so intense, I didn't actually enjoy it all that much. Her ass felt amazing, but my climax was akin to slamming my fist into a brick wall. Feels good to let out all that steam, not so good on the knuckles.

Withdrawing from her, I stumble back and collect my senses. Wiping off my cock, I pull up my pants and survey her, her wrists still tied to the exposed pipes of the basement we're in, her dress bunched up about her hips, her panties wrapped below her ass, my cum dripping down her thighs.

The nice thing, the loving thing, to do is untie her, wrap my arms about her, the way I used to after we'd had sex, hold her and see to her aftercare if we had an intense play session.

But that was before she left me.

It took me over two years to track her down. Partly because I had wasted time barking up the wrong tree. I thought maybe she had gotten together again with her ex-boyfriend, Dante. And maybe she had, though he swore they hadn't seen each other in years, but it took a little while to convince me that they were no longer together. After exhausting Amy's family, the two other women Bridget had shared an apartment with, instructors, and classmates at Cal, came the arduous task of tracking down a woman named Coretta.

You did a good job making it hard for me to find you, I compliment Bridget as I eye her rump, still flush from the spanking I gave her with my wet shirt. That delicious ass has been on the receiving end of many different implements: the paddle, a tawse, the flogger, and even a bouquet of nettles. I want the chance to apply all those things to her backside again.

But does she want it?

She did come on my cock, but that doesn't mean she wants to be with me.

Turning her to face me, I grab her jaw, which pushes up her cheeks. "You came without permission, Bridge."

"I'm—I'm sorry," she stutters.

"You know better than that."

She lowers her lashes. I hate that she still looks attractive to me, especially with her cheeks flushed from having just come.

"What's the matter?" I ask. "You out of practice?"

She looks at me with emotions too mixed for me to figure out. "Yes. I—I haven't been with anyone…"

I snort. "You expect me to believe you?"

Glancing down briefly, she doesn't object right away. That upsets me.

I reach between her legs. "Who'd you give my pussy to?"

Her lashes flutter as I stroke her flesh.

"Who'd you get wet for?" I ask.

She moans before answering, "No one."

"No one? What about Dante?"

She looks distressed.

235

"Thought so," I say with anger as I rub her clitoris.

A few minutes later, she starts to whimper and squirm. Withdrawing my fingers, I place them in her mouth. She knows to suck my digits clean. My cock stiffens at the suction upon my fingers.

But first, there's the matter of her punishment.

I tear off her panties, a flimsy and somewhat old pair. I bought her nice underwear when she was with me, but she doesn't want to have anything to do with me. Opening her mouth, I shove the panties between her lips. Stepping away, I look around and see cords of rope hanging on one wall. I pick a monofilament polypropylene rope. My favorite is jute, but this will still work well. After unwinding the rope, I tie a knot into it. I wrap the rope about her hips and between her legs, securing the knot right at her clit. Taking another cord of rope, I bend one of her legs, bind her ankle to the top of the thigh, and slip the rope under her knee before tossing it over a pipe overhead. With one leg hoisted in the air, she wobbles on her standing leg. The high heels she has on don't help.

Good.

Grabbing my wet shirt, I look at her one last time before heading out and closing the basement door behind me.

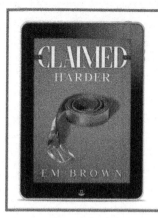

Made in the USA
Monee, IL
16 July 2021

73742271R00134